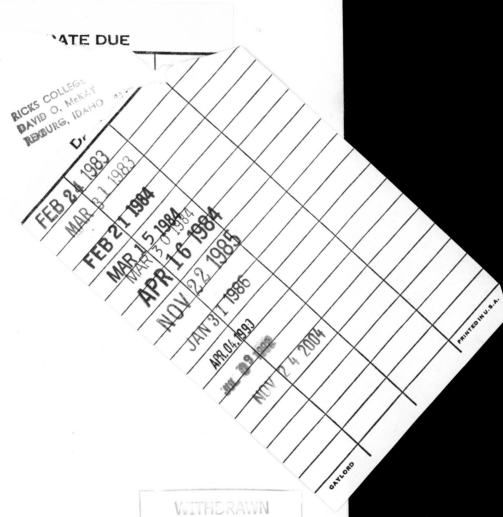

CHRYSALIS

Joyce Ellen Davis

CHRYSALIS

by

Joyce Ellen Davis

Olympus Publishing Company
1670 East Thirteenth South
Salt Lake City, Utah 84105

Utah Arts Council
617 East South Temple
Salt Lake City, Utah 84111

Cover photograph and design by Tony Anderson
Edited and designed by Heather Bennett

Library of Congress Catalog Card Number 80-84927
International Standard Book Number 0-913420-91-3
Printed in the United States of America

For the people who,
like Victor Hugo's bird,
feel the limb give way beneath them,
yet sing,
knowing they have wings.

And for Bethany,
because.

one

MONDAY MORNING. OUT in the early morning traffic, the fox-hunting, deer-stalking, big-game traffic. It must have reached 90 degrees already. Funny, that in this noise and heat I should be thinking of a song I learned in the third grade: *White coral bells upon a slender stalk, lillies-of-the-valley grace my garden walk.*

I have not felt well lately. Nothing definite, just a sort of fatigue, an irritation. The doctor will probably tell me I have some terrible illness. Maybe it's the heat I feel popping like electricity through my body. If only the current in my head would turn off.

The doctor said it's only nerves, it's all in my mind. I am not sick at all. He removed a little mole from my right shoulder and gave me some large yellow pills, *tranquilizers!* My family will be spared the calm but dramatic scene I had planned. Mark will not whisk me off on a whirlwind cruise.

I will not languish on the deck of a Marjorca-bound ocean liner. But I can't help wondering what it's like to feel yourself dying. And whether there is really an afterlife. And if all the hymns and prayers and baptisms are meaningless. I think of the earnest tears I shed over uncountable cats and dogs and birds that died somewhere back in my childhood.

Nerves, popping like firecrackers. I've just finished reading DeFoe's *Journal of the Plague Year,* replete with buboes and fevers and ravings. There are no crazy people in my family. Until now. They all have clean red blood and rosy cheeks. Not one of them has ever even noticed *nerves.* I make a mental note of my own particular soundness. I'll not be going to the pesthouse today, dear Mark.

Poor Mark, studying to be an anthropologist, trying to go to school, and work, and feed and clothe a hypochondriac wife and four noisy babies. His magazines and newspapers pile up unread, I guess because of all the other reading he has to do. The desk is piled with thick, dull-colored volumes entitled *Antiquity of Man, Fossil Man, The Evolution of Palaeolithic Cultures,* etc., all appropriately illustrated with drawings and photographs of flint scrapers, hand axes, bone chips and skulls.

Poor Mark. I will try to quiet the babies, and keep up with the ironing so his shirts won't look so rumpled when he leaves for work. He is in the bathroom. He calls, "Jody?"

"What are you doing in there?" I knock on the bathroom door.

"Nothing."

"Are you reading?"

"No." He is silent a minute, then he asks, "How are you, honey?"

"Fine, I guess. Guess what the doctor said?"

"You're pregnant." Pause.

"No. I have nerves."

"Nerves?" he says, with a capital N.

"I am nervous. That's what's the matter with me. He took a mole off my arm, too."

"You don't look nervous," he says.

·　·　·　·

Wednesday. Mark has taped a message to the telephone, marked URGENT. The doctor wants me to call back immediately, which I do. I talk to the nurse. She says nothing except that Doctor Sontag wants to see me. She will not tell me why. Secret messages make me nervous. I swallow a yellow pill before I go.

Doctor Sontag seems surprised to see me. "Oh, Jody," he says, looking somewhat nervous himself, "It's you. Somehow I didn't connect this with you." Connect *what* with me? "Sit down." He ushers me to a swivel rocking chair in his office, and he sits across from me. "I have some bad news," he begins.

He tells me that I have cancer—malignant melanoma, a particularly rapid and virulent, deadly form of cancer—in the mole he removed from my shoulder. I don't cry. I don't even blink. They want to operate soon, tomorrow or the next day. He wants to remove part of my arm, to make a "wide re-excision." He speaks of deranged cells, lymphatics, metastasis, of skin grafts from my thigh. He says, "Pathology indicates the melanoma cells are in an invasive state," looking at his hands as he speaks, and not at me. He shows me the pathologist's report.

3

But I'm too young, I remind myself in protest. I have just had a baby. I have little children at home. My ears are ringing so loudly I can't hear what else he says, but I continue to follow his moving lips.

It should make a difference. But it doesn't. There is a growing fist of ice blocking my breath. My lungs ice over. I can't swallow, or see, or think. Nothing moves but the doctor's lips. The moment is frozen. It's not fair. *It's not fair.*

· · · ·

All the hospital lights are on. I feel terribly sick. Somehow I have contracted hepatitis. They've had to postpone the operation until the infection is gone. I swallow twice to keep from throwing up. In a panic I put out my hand and touch the cold, unfamiliar railing at the side of the bed.

"Hello," Mark smiles. I glance at the wall clock. It is a little after five. A.M. or P.M.? "You'll only be here a short time. It won't be so bad," he tells me.

My God, I am dying and he says it won't be so bad. He holds my hand. "How are you?"

"I'm okay, I guess."

It's a lie. I keep shivering with fever and throwing up. A nurse pulls the curtain around my bed. There are other patients in the room who do not need to see this spectacle. The hours melt into each other, day or night. I sleep a lot, and wake up only when they want to stick me with another needle. I have strange fever dreams. I dream I have written a book, and I call it *The Black Boy and the Preacher's Snot.* I can't imagine what deranged microbes inspired this book. The title reminds me of Dylan Thomas's "When I was a windy boy and a bit, and the black spit of the chapel fold . . . sighed the old ramrod, dying . . ."

Dying. *I hope I am not dying.*

A whole band, crashing cymbals, timpani, tubas and trumpets and all, marches through my dreams, their golden epaulets waving and brass buttons shining. "What band is that?" I ask.

"That," someone says, "is the Kahntoum Hamish Duck Band."

Mark says he must go and relieve the baby-sitter. "Shall I call your folks and tell them?" he asks.

"Tell them *what*? That I have cancer. No."

"They ought to know."

"You mean before they read it in the obituaries?" I am embarrassed. I would feel the same embarrassment had I been told I have gonorrhea. "Why do they have to know?"

"Because they love you."

"Then tell them . . . I'm sick. I'll tell them the rest when it's over. I don't want them to worry."

"All right," he says, "I'll see you later."

A nurse comes in and makes notes on a yellow pad at the bottom of the bed. I cough.

"Do you feel like throwing up again?"

No. There is nothing left to throw up. I still can't swallow. I have not been able to eat or drink. They've x-rayed my brain, my lungs, they've filled me with radio-active dye and scanned my liver, and they've taken enough blood to build a Frankenstein.

This cancer is an intruder. It has entered my life quietly, skulking behind my baby. While the child inside me sprouted his fingers and toes, while his ribs and vertebrae turned to bone, this black thing sprouted and grew. *Nothing*

5

will ever be the same again.

I've never been sick before. My experience with hospitals is limited to the optimism of the maternity ward. But this is another kind of place. An old woman sleeps in the bed next to mine. Hanging bottles and threading tubes lace in and out of her every orifice. The fluid eventually drains from her into a bag at the foot of her bed or empties efficiently into the colostomy pouch at her side. I, too, am connected to an intravenous bottle and tube. The needle goes in near my wrist.

My folks have sent flowers. I can't tell them yet.

Six-thirty A.M. They come in and take me to X-ray again, the portable IV swinging along as we go down the elevator. Last time I moved and the film blurred. We have to do it over again. How can they expect me to lie here so long without moving? I have to cough. I have to go to the bathroom. I'm going to throw up again. There go the pictures. Damn! I'm tired and I'm angry. I want to go back to sleep.

I dream of riding a great slow horse through an open place. There is much light where he walks, but the light illumines nothing. Where are we? The light widens into a river. We walk out toward the center. I can feel the bottomless light beneath us, as deep as the horse's flanks in places, or else impassable. I am frightened and confused. I lie curled against the animal for comfort, my hands grip his mane, but I fall. I cry out.

A hand touches my shoulder. "You all right?" Mark.

"I'm all right," I mumble. "I'm fine." Majorca, here I come.

two

THE HEPATITIS IS GONE.
Fever is gone. They have rescheduled my operation for next week. I am scared. I try not to think of this—thing—crawling, multiplying, penetrating the blood and lymph streaming to my lungs or brain.

"Normal cells stick to each other. A kidney cell stays in the kidney where it belongs, and a lung cell stays in the lung. But cancer cells have no home," Doctor Sontag had once said. "Melanoma cells tend to become rapidly invasive. Theoretically the change is reversible, but at the present time we just don't know how."

Don't know how. Why the hell not? They can send men to the moon, they can measure the vibration of molecules, they can divide time to the ten trillionth of a trillionth of a second, they have annihilated smallpox! They don't know how? *Why not?*

Since the operation is postponed until next week I can go home for the weekend. Hurrah!

There is much hugging and kissing.

"Would you like to go out for dinner?" Mark asks, in a festive mood.

"Fine." I've been sprung, if not pardoned. At least the execution has been put off. We take the kids to McDonald's for dinner. It is delicious—the taste and smell and feel of hamburgers and onions, and french fries, and grease, the sound of people eating and talking and laughing together.

"Guess what I did today, Mama!" My four-year-old, Chris says he called Grandma on the telephone. Grandma lives in California. Oh no.

"You didn't!" I say.

"Yes, I did! I talked to Grandma, and Grandma says to me, she said 'This . . . is . . . a . . . recording.'"

We all laugh. It feels so *good*.

After dinner, when the boys have gone to sleep, we make love.

"I missed you," Mark says, tracing a featherlight trail with his finger down my ribs to a sizable bump of hipbone where there didn't used to be a hipbone. "Ticklish?"

"You don't waste time, do you?" A quick shiver. "There's plenty of time."

Yesterday I met a man dying of lung cancer. He said his wife won't kiss him anymore for fear of catching it. It had never occurred to me that Mark might be afraid to touch me. He's not. When we lie relaxed in each other's arms, I discover I still wear this wretched plastic bracelet that links me to the hospital. I cut it loose and throw it in the trash. I'm sure they'll find me another.

Mark wrote me fantastic love letters before we were married. I was touring with the American Repertory Players much of the time, doing one-night stands, living in hotels while he worked as a counselor in a home for emotionally disturbed children. He wrote:

Meine Lieb, Ich habe Einsamkeit, Ich bin sehr einsam. I love you, oh how I love you. It's very hard to be separated from you so much.

I was beginning to worry about getting away for the weekend, however we're supposed to lose six children tomorrow. This will relieve a lot of pressure all around. I worked with the toddlers today—18 kids with runny noses. I'm sure I must've caught something.

I want to be with you. I want to touch you. I'd like to go to sleep next to your warm, soft body. Wow! You should've tuned in on my dream last night. I wrote you a love letter as sexy as any Balzac could have thought up. The poetry was beautiful. Just think—in a few more days I'll be with you for hundreds of hours. You ought to see my bed— littered with letters, books and magazines. I just sort of burrow a place to sleep.

The air is full of orange blossoms and sea smells. Warm days and blue skies.

Good night, my love, good night.
I miss the warmth I wish were mine.

Mark

To which I replied:

Mon bien aimee, mon cher—
Oh, the snow and the ice and the cold outside! The more it snows, the more it goes, the more it goes on snowing! And nobody knows, how cold my toes, how cold my toes are growing. Tiddley pom.

I can hardly lift my feet in these snow boots. If I slip, I'll never get up. Like a ladybug turned upside down. Would you believe it if I told you all the fingers of my left hand fell off this morning when I removed my glove? No, I didn't think you would. However, the whole world is white and cold in spite of what you tell me. So I'll be there soon to see for myself. *Presque aussitot. Tout de suite.*

I love you. I LOVE you. I love YOU. Take your pick. take two, they're small . . .

Forever and ever,
Jody

To which he replied:

I picked all three . . .

Monday morning we drive back to the hospital.

"Hey," says Mark. "You're crying."

"I am not. I never cry."

"You know I love you, Jo."

"I love you, too."

I don't want to have to come back here to this dreary place. This is not the way it's supposed to be. *Please, please don't leave me here again!*

"Do you want me to go up with you?" Mark kisses me good-bye at the elevator.

"No. I'll be all right," I lie. What a long day this is going to be.

• • • •

In celebration of Operation Day they rout me from my bed at four A.M. and send me to the shower. I have never liked rising at four A.M., or showering. I polished my fingernails last night so they wouldn't cut my arm off. It made sense at the time. The polish was my last hook in the real world of order and poise and planning. My last defense. They make me remove it so they can check my circulation after I am unconscious. No mysteries here. If the tissue under the nail turns blue . . .

In this alcove off the operating room, a lovely girl with a malignant brain tumor is being prepared for surgery. They have shaved her head and anesthetized her. She is very young. Sleeping, she looks like a beautiful pink baby with her bald head. She wears a wedding ring, and I wonder if she has babies of her own. They wheel her away. I think there is not much hope.

I spoke to her sister yesterday. The girl had surgery a couple of months ago. They removed a substantial part of the tumor, but new growth rapidly filled up the cavity. This operation may restore her normal functions again for another month, but she will die in any event. The tumor will expand to press against her skull, and when that happens, her death will be swift.

At six A.M. a young anesthesiologist comes in and gives me a shot, a sedative. "How's it going?" he asks brightly.

"As soon as you leave," I tell him, "I'm going out the window and never coming back." He laughs. He thinks I am kidding.

Patients like to believe their doctors are infallible. A tall doctor I have never seen stops by my bed. I spin in slow circles, bed and all.

"Mrs. Harper," he says in his most reassuring voice, "I am Doctor Cutler. I will be assisting Doctor Sontag with your surgery." He reviews my chart and begins a meticulous inspection of my left arm. He scratches some notes on the chart and puts it on the nightstand. There is much information on the chart. What is most interesting is that he has written something about my *left* arm. *Should I tell him it's my right arm they're fixing,* I wonder drowsily? I tell him.

He looks at his watch, clears his throat, and smiles. "Of course," he says. He hides his embarrassment well.

Doctors don't know everything.

The operation is over. I can't seem to find my voice, and my throat feels like I swallowed a box of cotton. They didn't have to do a skin graft after all, but they painted me with iodine from ear to knee just in case. Now I am bandaged from neck to elbow. All this because of one small spot. One small, dark spot and I am alien. I feel like someone else. Like Job, I walk upon a snare, waiting to be caught.

I am sleepy. They come in and take my temperature and blood pressure readings, first at fifteen-minute intervals, now at half-hour intervals. Whenever I shut my eyes I swim in a fog of nitrous oxide and pentothal. The sea is scarlet and unbelievably brilliant. Scalpels and hemostats flash. The melanoma looks like an *eye* floating in a glass jar. *What an evil thing.* There is lots of blood.

"Just one more time, honey," says a nurse as she tightens the pressure cuff, "and we'll wheel you back to your own room."

This is not my own room. My own room has a dusty, sunny smell. There are pictures on the walls. The bed is wide and soft, and the sheets are printed with lavender flowers. This room is definitely someplace else.

Annelise, my friend from next door comes. She sits on the edge of the bed. Conspicuously worried, she views my bulky arm, with its ominous wrappings, and warns "Be careful. Cancer *kills.*"

As if I didn't know. *Nerd.* "I will. Thanks, Annie." Does she think I can choose to be careless? I feel angry again. I wish she'd leave now. *Go away, Annie!*

I want to go home. I want to go for a walk in the hills. I want it to rain all over me and wash off all the hospital smell. I want to hold my babies. I want to be alive. I want to celebrate.

The Eye in the Bottle

The first eye
A cat's eye
In a bottle
Can be
dissected
In a matter of minutes
Revealing
Optic nerve
Cornea
Lens and
Iris
All innocence.

The second eye
Blind
Floating
In its alcohol bath
Proves
When dissected
(Laid open on the table)
To be deadly:
Provoking
Worms in the apples
That bruise the flesh
And spoil the barrel.
Double helix of

Unfit spirals
Out of gear, dangling . . .
Deficient chromosomes and genes
Locks
Without keys
Generating
Inherited distempers among
The blind
The epileptic
The diabetic
The cancerous
The insane.

The third eye
The mind's eye is
Exempt
From eugenics, is
Exempt
From innocence or guilt and
Will not simply
Endure,
It will
Prevail.

three

I HAVE A NEW ROOM-mate, besides frail old Mrs. Fische and her bottles and tubes. Directly across from me, surrounded by three large vases of flowers and several smaller ones, is an elderly lady named Tillie, who has had an eye operation to restore her sight. She is supposed to lie still, but she doesn't. She must have a cigarette so she puts on her high-heeled shoes. Maybe she needs to dress up for Mr. Fische, who is her smoking buddy at least twice a day. Her blue and white hospital gown is open down the back and her fanny is bare. Her heels clatter on the tiles and her gown flaps open like a flag. She must be seventy. Maybe she's a retired hooker—I haven't seen so many flowers since Mark's Uncle Frank died at a hundred and one. Mr. Fische is late today so she stops by my bed to chat. She's really into English history. She says, "Ethelred was King in 978. He always did the wrong thing."

Poor Ethelred.

"Edward the Confessor was his son." She goes on and

on: William I, William II, Henry I, Henry II, Richard I, and John. A nurse comes by and tells Tillie to go back to bed. The nurse has brought grape juice on a tray, but Tillie won't allow any help and she pours the dark juice all over her gown and sheets. The nurse is angry. Poor Tillie. Poor Ethelred. Poor nurse who has to change the purple sheets and the wet gown. Poor, poor Mrs. Fische. Poor, poor me. I turn toward the wall and shut my eyes.

Doctor Sontag comes in. He is no older than I, his face is unwrinkled, his hair is blond. He might be my brother. "Jody? Are you sleeping?" he asks.

Too bad if I am. "No." I sit up in bed. "This is a terrible pillow! I think it's full of straw."

"I'll have them send you up another. Outside of that, how are you feeling?"

"Fine, except for this frog in my throat."

"Say, 'Ahhh.'" He looks down my throat. "You're right. It is a frog. A little green one!"

Good Lord, he's a comedian, too. I smile. Better be polite or he'll tell me something else to cheer me up. He wants me to know why he considered the skin graft unnecessary. He has performed a six-inch "z-plasty" instead. Then, shyly proud of his own ingenuity, he confesses: he has experimented on my arm. I am fastened together with— among other things—tongue depressors! *Dr. Cutler's idea perhaps.* When he is ready to leave, he adds casually, "By the way, the lab tests showed nothing residual!"

My heart leaps. "Then is it over?"

He is cautious. "I don't know. We'll just have to wait and see."

"But will it come back?"

"With this type of malignancy recurrences are common."

"How common?" I persist.

He hesitates, clearly wondering how candid he ought to

be with me. He says, "Of the 5,000 people who develop malignant melonoma each year, 4,000 will die, most of them very quickly. Some slower growing tumors will go into remission, reappearing as long as twenty years after the initial lesion."

I wish I hadn't asked. The lump of fear in my stomach rises to my throat. I wish he had said, "Yes, it is over. Go home, live long, and be happy." I wish I were someplace else, anywhere else. The statistical probability is that I will die "very quickly." And deep down, I refuse to believe any of it. Instead, I wrap myself in a cocoon and behave as if these things will not happen to me. After all, the tests showed nothing residual—that leaves some spark of hope. Maybe I will be among the lucky 1,000. Maybe I won't. Nothing is sure.

·　·　·　·

Mrs. Fische died today. I think I am going to cry. I feel a great loss although I didn't know her really. We spoke only once, when she asked me, "Are the holidays here yet?"

The nurse checked her pulse, disconnected the IV, stored it neatly in the corner, and pulled the curtain. Much later, a doctor arrived with another man in a dark business suit. They brought a gurney and a large gold cloth that looked like a tablecloth. After a few minutes they emerged, wheeling the gurney out. The bed was empty.

She's better off, I say to myself. What a depressing place. I think I'll go upstairs and look at the new babies. The nurses won't like that. I'll pretend I'm going down to the solarium, and when no one is looking, I'll dash into the elevator. With my robe on and my wood and stainless-steel bionic arm covered up, no one will know. They'll think I'm one of the mothers.

From one of the labor rooms I hear a woman crying for a drink of water. I pass her door quickly, but I notice her hair is wild and her eyes are frightened. At least she'll have something to show for this visit. She'll have a baby and I'll have a six-inch scar.

"They all look like Woody Woodpecker to me," Mark had said the night our first son was born.

The contractions came at increasingly frequent intervals, my abdomen hard, then soft again. Between times I tried to read from a book I had brought: "Three or four days after birth, a fluid called colostrum comes from the breast. It differs from the real milk which usually appears. . . ." I closed the book and held my breath against the pain that began again in my back and crawled up and over the mountain in the middle of me.

"Is it bad?" Mark said, slipping a pillow under my back.

"What's a little excruciating pain?" I tried to laugh, thinking never, never again will I repeat this performance. It wasn't fair that I should have to endure this while Mark sat calmly in the chair by the bed. I grasped for his hand. "Just hold on. Tighter. Yes, like that. Oh!"

I relaxed just a little. "There. I made it through another one. Wow!" I tried the book again. ". . . on the third or fourth day. Most physicians will put the baby to the breast sometime during the first twenty-four hours after—" I stopped reading and dropped the book to the bed, thinking *nothing, nothing is worth this pain. I'm so tired.* I tried a joke. "I think I've changed my mind. I don't want a baby after all." Bad joke.

A smiling nurse arrived, lifted my gown and stabbed me with a needle. With the edges of pain dulled, I dozed. *I know you, I've lived with you for nine months.* Two masked nurses wheeled me to the table and Mark smiled, assuring me he was there, that everything was all right. I saw myself in a mirror, spread into the stirrups, beside a huge round fluorescent light.

"Push!" Doctor Sontag's voice came from the bottom of a well. "Push! Look, the head's crowning."

"I *am* pushing, dammit." I said indignantly, pushing. I half sat up. In the mirror I saw the baby's head, dark and glistening.

"Don't stop pushing."

Then he was there, sliding out of my flesh, crying, wet. I stared at him. My son. His eyes were puffy and closed. His skin was a little blue and his head was elongated and crooked. The doctor cut the umbilical cord, and if he were ever truly a part of me, my son was now wholly himself. He lay across my stomach making little swimming, crawling movements, his fingers curling delicately over his palms.

I felt incredible relief. And euphoria—lifting me higher than I'd ever been before. I soared. "Mark, he's magnificent! He looks just like you!"

"He looks like Woody Woodpecker," said Mark.

They all do. I can hear them crying through the nursery window.

"Which one is yours?" A young woman in a bright silk kimono and furry slippers asks me, her reflection smiling out of the glass.

"I'm sorry. Did you speak to me?"

"I said, which one is yours?"

19

"None of them are mine. I—I have four boys at home," I add apologeticaly, as if that justifies my being up here. "I belong downstairs—Which one is yours?"

Back in my room I find an orderly has brought Tillie a new pillow.

•   •   •   •

"Did you hear," Mark asks, "about the man who dreamed he ate a ten pound marshmallow, and when he woke up his pillow was gone?"

"Yes, I've heard that one before."

"Aha! Well, my dear, how about this one? What's green, and barks?"

"All right. What?" I say grudgingly.

"Lassie, the. avocado!" He pokes a finger at my ribs. "Don't let a smile crease your face! Down with mirth! What's black and white and gray?"

"Stop it. Stop it!" I'm giggling in spite of myself. "What in the world are you doing?"

"I'm going to tickle you to death, my dear."

"With all this disease around, who needs it?"

"What's black and white and gray?"

"I don't know. Stop that! What if the nurse should come in?"

"Had enough? Come on, give up?"

"I give up!"

"Sister Mary Elephant."

"They're going to think you've escaped from the psychiatric ward. You know, you could have a terrific future in comedy—you and Doctor Sontag and William F. Buckley."

"Hey, you're finally smiling. It's about time, my dear!" Mark draws the curtain around the bed. "This is a private party," he says, winking at Tillie.

I'm glad he is here. His W. C. Fields act is terrible, but I'm lonely and tired of being brave. *Make it better, Mark.* Make it like it was before. I've tried TV: Popeye at seven A.M., the game shows, the talk shows, the soaps. I even tried to listen when Tillie told me about Queen Victoria and Prince Albert of Saxe-Coburg-Gotha.

•　　•　　•　　•

At last I can go home—to my own house, my own bathroom and kitchen, my own bed. I can use my arm to write, to lift my fork to my mouth. I can't raise it high enough to comb my hair, or wash it, but these things I can do one-handed, left-handed, awkwardly. I'll look like the Witch of the West for a couple of weeks. So what.

I can go home, and I need not return for two weeks, and then only to have the stitches removed. After that, I need not return for three months! *Three months.* Ninety days without needles or tubes, without the indignity of pain—or the intrusion of dying.

I can go home to Mark and my babies and my own dear pillow.

four

MY LITTLE BOYS ARE
glad I'm home. They've drawn some funny crayon pictures
for me—of themselves, long-legged and round-headed, of
the family going for an outing in the car, all smiles, and of
our house suspended in the air atop the sidewalk like a
popsicle on a stick, all pink and green and yellow.

There is some sweet with all the bitter: I lost seventeen
pounds in fourteen days!

There is little pain. Mark brings me books and flowers.
The neighbors bring casseroles and cakes. They whom I love
have not turned against me. I'm not yet as Job. I try to be
cheerful, but my head is still somewhere else. I need breathing time, stillness, a prayer to lift me above fear.

Will there really be a morning?
  Is there such a thing as day?
Could I see it from the mountains
  If I were as tall as they?

Has it feet like water-lillies?
  Has it feathers like a bird?
Is it brought from famous countries
  Of which I have never heard?

Oh, some scholar! Oh, some sailor!
  Oh, some wise man from the skies!
Please to tell a little pilgrim
  Where the place called morning lies.*

*Emily Dickinson

• • • •

We take a ride in the car, and I roll my window down so I can feel the wind, so I can give the day to all my senses. The air smells like peppermint. My lord, what a morning! I should have been a gypsy. Here, little pilgrims, is the place where morning lies. In these patchwork hills is all the light, the gold and orange of morning.

We stop and eat apples in the hush of aspens that do not quake and the scarlet of scrub oak. We admire the occasional lizards that run among the roots. Ants are everywhere.

It is not frost that turns these leaves to vermilion, but a subtle change in the internal chemistry of each leaf. In summer, the leaf prepares for its own death by forming a light ridge of cells at the base of its stem. Beneath this layer of cells, another layer will form to heal the scar when the leaf dies and falls.

I remember names of things I have not thought of since I was in school—gymnosperm, chlamydemonas, gloecapsa, oscillatoria, nostoc, anabaena, earth stars and destroying angels. All my bells are ringing. Downy mildew of grape, white rust and red summer rust. But too soon I am tired and we have to go home. We gather the brightest leaves to take with us.

I keep touching the babies. I love their softness, the clean smell of them. We all pile into the bed after celebrating the day with hot chocolate and cinnamon toast, and we count our leaves. We read "Whose Mouse Are You?" and "Fish Is Fish." They are beautiful children, spectacularly beautiful, with long lashes and sky-blue eyes, and thick, dark brows like Mark's.

"What time is it?" Remy asks, yawning.

"It's almost bedtime."

"Do you have a watch?"

"No."

"Where is your Mickey Mouse one? Is it broke?"

"Yes, I guess it is. Are you ready to go to bed?"

"Yep. Do you know what? Elephants have great big watches," he says.

"Do they?"

"Do you know what else?"

"No, what?" I suspect he is stalling. I don't mind.

"The moon has no nose. It doesn't."

"I suppose not. You're right. But it has in pictures sometimes."

"Yes. Pictures lie. Do you know what else?"

"Have you brushed your teeth?"

"Yes. Buffalos have no bumpers. Now I'll read to you."

He finds a book he has brought home from school, and reads with a slight lisp. "Make a house, Ned. Make a big house. A big, big house."

Near Christmas, on a snowy hilltop we hiked to one Sunday afternoon before we were married, Mark asked me what things I wanted. I said, "I want to have someplace of my own, and somebody to come to, and a big house with a fireplace and a king-size bed, and babies with soft flannel pajamas. And a maid. And a chauffeur and a cook. . . ."

Now I can do without the chauffeur and the maid. A cook and a king-size bed would be nice.

It's so good to be home, to touch, to be touched. How good it is!

I've become intensely aware of my body. I am a little paler, and thinner. I love to feel my flat abdomen. My baby is only three months old and my tummy hasn't been this flat in a long time. I pour a lot of Emeraude and bubblebath into the bathwater. I undress and run my hands over my body, feeling very female. I'm glad I lost that seventeen pounds. Steam rises and fogs the mirror. It is now that I notice new spots, ones I don't remember having seen before. I am suddenly fearful, suspicious of every one. Horrified, I stare at a black spot on my foot. *Not again, oh, please not again!* My stomach knots and churns, and I have to throw up. Thank God the running water muffles the sound.

The black spot on my foot washes off in the bath and floats away between the bubbles. I laugh at myself until the laughter changes to tears. Is this how it will be for the rest of my life? I really am becoming some kind of a nut! I must not let this sort of hysteria control me. I must memorize every spot, not missing even *one* so that I'll know for sure. Every contour and line must become as familiar to me as constellations in the night sky. Here, on my left shoulder blade is my Polaris. Here Orion, here Draco the Dragon. . . . Now breathe deeply, and the shivering will stop. Still shaking, I manage to knock the perfume bottle off the edge of the shelf, and it shatters, spilling Emeraude over everything. I'm making enough noise to wake up the whole house.

"Are you okay?" Mark calls.

"I just broke a bottle."

"So I heard. Good news travels fast."

"They call me Grace," I say, "but not too often."

"They do?"

They say that a dying person's life flashes before his eyes in the space of a few minutes, through the fourth dimension into the fifth, in the time it takes to blink. Lying in the bed, in the dark, I am six years old again, watching snakes climb up the gray folds in the window-curtains, hearing the old photographs on the walls whisper to one another of times past in quiet, paper voices. My heart thumps monstrously loud.

Whatever happened to Baby Dumpling and the rocking chair, and all those pop-bottles full of sand? Nicodemus had no shoes, so who was it stepped in everybody's pie? Jesus loves me, this I know. I'll be a sunbeam for Him. I love Jesus. I love cats. Cue-ball is my cat. He rides in the little buggy and sings. A sunbeam, a sunbeam, Jesus wants me for a sunbeam. *Loves*. By pinching is how people who love each other very much get babies.

I was stunned when mother told me how people *do* get babies. "Do you remember that word I told you not to say?" Mother must have been acutely embarrassed. "*That's* what people do." She never said *the word*, but that was my sex education. I knew these bizarre activities occurred, whatever they were called. But I could not imagine why anyone would want to do such things, and certainly, if they did, it didn't concern me. We never talked about "it" again.

Mark's breathing becomes deep and regular. He is asleep. Why can't I sleep? I trace his eyebrows with my finger, but he doesn't wake. I love you. I love you. *Everything is going to be all right now, isn't it, Mark?*
Please.

> *As long*
> *as you hold on to me,*
> *as long*
> *as I can feel your arm across me*
> *in the night*
> *when the night wears thin,*
> *the delicate dream persists.*

•   •   •   •

My little Chris hates being alone. All day he hugs my legs and pulls on my clothes. He sleeps in our bed, he wants me to be with him every minute. I think my stay in the hospital was more damaging to him than to the rest of us. I should have said something to him before I left, but it all happened too fast. What were the words I should've said?

He won't let me out of his sight, he follows me from room to room. If I go into the bathroom and close the door, he waits impatiently, calling "Mama, are you in there?" If he comes into a room and I am not immediately in sight he bursts into tears. At bedtime, kissing my face as I kiss his, he begs me not to "go anywhere," and he asks where I will be while he is sleeping. For Chris, especially, I have to stay well!

He told me this story called The Cat in the Window: "Once upon a time there was a cat was in the window, and he was sad, and he kept looking for his mother because he was lonely. But his mother never came back, because she was dead."

Two o'clock in the morning and sleep won't come. But I ought to sleep so that I can take the boys to the library today.

The ritual is to spend Tuesday mornings in the public library, where they offer a pre-school story hour, and I have the hour for myself. I read all I can find concerning cancer, melanoma in particular. Everything I know about my illness I discover during these hours alone, and all of it is horrid and terrifying and impersonal. I know the odds are not good.

I read: A melanoma is a tumor which contains melanin, the dark pigment found in the skin, hair, and eyes. This cancer ordinarily begins as a small irregularly-shaped growth that's bluish-black or dark brown. Sometimes it has no color at all. Most often it occurs in a mole or other birthmark. It gets steadily larger and may bleed after the slightest injury. The lymphatic system is the main invasion route of melanomas. Through these underground channels melanomas spread rapidly to the lungs, brain, or other vital organs.

I read of the excision of lymph nodes and surrounding tissue, of B.C.G. injections and immunotherapy, of perfusion techniques, and of the amputation of limbs.

I read optimistic autobiographies and journals of other people who've shared their experiences with cancer—most of which, I note with interest, were published *posthumously.*

Melampus said moles reveal hidden things and profound mysteries. Moles, he wrote, are the stars of the human being, encircling our bodies as the stars and planets encircle the universe. A mole on a woman's forehead denotes power. Moles on the lip betray gluttony. Upon the nape of the neck, however, the beauty spot predicts decapitation. On the shoulder, captivity and unhappiness. Melampus was an astrologer. Fortunately, I do not believe in astrology.

I can never admit being afraid. I never talk about IT to anyone. The subject of cancer, like the subject of sex when I was a child, is avoided. Everyone (including me) wears a mask that smiles continuously.

I can't talk to Mark, nor to my friends, nor even my doctor. We discuss neutron stars, parapsychology, football, Bartok, the weather, pyramid power, biofeedback, Chris's bad dreams, but we do not discuss cancer. I am afraid to talk about it, as if the words themselves might come crashing down upon me like giant hailstones, as if saying (or hearing) them will suddenly materialize all their unbodied horrors. I am afraid and anxious and angry and concerned—and I want to know that people *care*, that they are concerned, too. Oh, I know they care by what they all *do* for me. But nobody ever *says* it. Maybe they are afraid of the words, too?

Never before have I felt so keenly the limits of mortality, the beginnings and the endings. What I need most is to know that someone will be there to hold my hand if I need it.

five

AT HALF PAST THREE ON the following Wednesday, I go to the clinic to have my stitches removed. The clinic is a most efficient place. Hospital routines are conducted with a minimum of fuss. An embroidered sampler hangs in the long white halls. It is a lovely old prayer used by Alcoholics Anonymous:

> God grant me the serenity
> to accept the things I cannot change,
> the courage to change the things I can,
> and the wisdom to know the difference.

I wait, and flip through six or eight magazines, pausing at the ads of beautiful people smiling above the terse warning of the surgeon general that cigarette smoking may be hazardous to health. A pretty red-haired lady wearing lots of green eye-shadow sits beside me. After a moment she inquires about my bionic arm. I tell her about the melanoma.

"Oh, really! My husband died of melanoma!" she says.

"He did?" I am shaken. I thought people only said that

in bad jokes: *My Uncle had what you have, and he lingered and lingered!* "Well," I say, "that's encouraging."

She is embarrassed. "But I didn't mean . . . I only . . . Oh, I'm so sorry. . . ."

"It's okay." But my heart is racing like mad. I have a lot of questions. I want to ask her how he died. What was it like? Was he in pain? A lot of pain? Did it last long? Lord, how long? But I don't ask any of these questions. "It must be hard for you to be alone now," I say.

"Yes. But I have my children."

"That's good." Thank God, it's my turn to go. She waves.

I unbutton my clothing and undress. I seem to have lost all modesty somewhere along the line. Lying naked on the table, I answer Doctor Sontag's questions about my general health while he launches an intense inspection of every square inch of skin. Dr. Frankenstein and his Monster. He feels for enlarged nodes in my neck and underarms before he begins to remove the piles of tape and gauze.

(I think of dying Mercutio's answer when Romeo tells him, "Courage, man. The hurt cannot be much."

"No, 'tis not so deep as a well, nor so wide as a church-door; but 'tis enough, 'twill serve. . . .")

There is a gaping hole. The place where my right shoulder ought to be is a canyon you could fall into. I was not prepared for this. The scar, a fat, purple caterpillar with countless steel legs, curls in an S from the south end of the canyon to the north end. I'm glad it's not on my face.

He removes the stitches gently, with skilled fingers. The wooden splints come away first. At a loss for words, I smile.

"A callepittar," I say stupidly. That's what Chris would call it.

"What's that?"

"I said it looks sort of like a caterpillar . . . but it's bigger than I thought it would be."

"Oh. Yes . . . that's a bad place for a scar." He beams, obviously pleased with the results of his stitchery. "You should've seen the size of the piece we took out."

My smile stays, but the rest of me races ahead on a stubborn joyless flight. The body is a fragile thing. Everything can't always be fixed, and some things cannot be changed, not for all our piety nor wit nor tears.

It is hard to think of dying. When death touches me, when it is *my* death, or the death of someone I love, only then do I truly feel the chilling grief and despair, only then do I vomit denials. Even if the cancer has left me, there are limits. And I have not put much time into examining my life, the way it could be, the way it was meant to be.

· · · ·

I listen to Berlioz' *Requiem* and write a long letter to my closest friend, Jennifer. She ought to know. How shall I say it? What are the words? Of all the things we've shared, this is most important. I know you won't know what to say, won't know what to do, but I have lots I wish we could talk about. I don't expect answers. If only we could touch one another . . . *if you could even cry with me.*

But she couldn't.

I didn't receive any letters of encouragement or consolation. There was a long, long silence. Finally she answered:

Dear, dear sweet Jody,

You are a friend, the only real one I've ever had, and I think you know that.

I wrote you a long letter about the period of time I spent worrying about you. I told Mark if you died, we would, of course, help with the kids. Never sent it. Mostly I just shut you off and out. I couldn't let myself think on that. Impossible. I'm sorry. I just couldn't handle it, so I shut you out.

The *Requiem* plays on, the four fortissimo brass bands and the kettle drums, Gabriel's trumpets, booming out doomsday.

six

IT IS AN EASY THING TO LIE
on the floor and do nothing, to lie in tight numbness and
think about nothing, to idle in neutral, waiting. I do not
think, I do not hope, I do not fear, I do not feel, I float on
the incensed air, the air of sandalwood and musk and rose.
It's an easy thing. Insensibility is simplicity.

I lie on the floor amid the crisscrossed flowers and light
green tendrils of the carpet, wrapped in stereo earphones,
and I lose myself in the bright coils and labyrinths and
elaborate mazes of Johann Sebastian Bach, "the Old Wig."

Ich Komme, dein teil
Ich warte mit brennendem Ole . . .
Komm Jesu! . . . Ich komme, Ich komme. . . .

The contrapuntal lines of the *Cantata* are tightly drawn
around the convolutions of my brain. They blend into the
six concerti dedicated to the Margrave of Brandenburg, the
Passacaglia in C-Minor and the *Goldberg Variations*:
majestic, over and over and over, the granite, indestructible

35

sounds, the arabesques of Bach.

Bach died blind, dictating the last of his music to his son-in-law. They say, in his final moments, faith triumphed over anguish, for he renamed the eighteen chorale preludes *Before Thy Throne, My God, I Stand.* He had first called them *When In The Hour of Direst Need.*

I am no longer concerned with lipstick or mascara. I do not bother to put on any make-up. When I look in the mirror I see there are dark shadows under my eyes. So?

When I do not lie on the floor bombarding all my senses with sound, I eat. I have gained back most of the seventeen pounds I lost. I seem determined to stuff myself to death, to fill an indescribable void. I'll eat anything that doesn't run away: cold spaghetti, soda crackers, dry bread, stale cake. I eat compulsively, without enjoyment. It doesn't even have to taste good. My complexion is going to pot. I hate myself. Why do I do this? I'm sorry, Mark, but I'm a mess of nerves. I'm a mess. I've been terrible today. Please forgive me if I'm difficult. I love you so much. I am sorry for you, for the boys, for myself, for the whole damn world.

But I am not part of the world. *Somewhere out there it must be Christmas.* There is a Christmas tree and snow, and Remy sings "Jingle Bells." I am separate. Christmas does not concern me this year. I munch a soda cracker and float away on the soft sandalwood air, a million miles away, ten million miles away from the familiar. It is so easy.

Memory is the real narcotic. A scene from another Christmas turns continuously in my head; it is the first Christmas Mark and I spend together. The silver icicles I have been hanging on the tree slip through my fingers onto the floor. I let them lie there. Mark kisses my neck, pushing me gently down upon the floor under the shining tree.

The shadows of the lights blinking across the ceiling and walls are red and black and gold, like stained glass. It is as though we lie in the center of a giant, pulsing throat, reflected in the concave bottoms of glass bells, in the convex bottoms of glass birds. It is very cold because they have shut off our gas, but we glow like the lights while the phonograph goes round and round with carols sung by the Mormon Tabernacle Choir. That Christmas I was pregnant with Remy, and didn't know it.

And all the Christmases after that one, filled with Beatrix Potter books and Mother Goose, alphabet blocks, tinker-toys and stuffed animals.

The scene shifts suddenly back to ME. I lie on the floor beside this Christmas tree and stare at my body. Monstrous black cells swarm, chewing my insides, expanding into thick, oozing sores, swelling, exploding into blood-red flowers that smell of death.

I sit up quickly and hug my knees. I can't go on thinking like this. A tear slides out and runs down my cheek. Remy comes to stand by me, draws his lips across my cheek briefly, and buries his nose in my hair.

•　•　•　•

At the rate my hair is falling out I'll be bald in a week. There's hair in the bed and hair on the floor, the drains are clogged with hair, great tangled gobs of hair. Will you love me when I'm old and gray? Will you love me when I'm *bald*?

Sometimes in the middle of the night (but never, never in daylight) I cry. I rock in the dark to the clock's ticking and feed the baby, and I cry. It's unfair that I might be cheated of his growing, of his going off to school. I cry for all those happy Christmas plays I'll miss—the children dressed in bells and tinsel, for the carols I won't hear sung. I cry for all the Easter baskets I won't fill with colored eggs and chocolate rabbits, for the pumpkin faces I won't see lighted. I cry for all the apples I won't pick from the tree, for the peaches and cherries I won't boil into jam. And yes, for all the illnesses of childhood I'll miss. I should be there for the fevers and coughs that will come with winters, to comfort, to assure. And, my dear Mark, I cry for the times I will not lie next to you and feel your arm across me in the dark, for the touching that will be gone. I cry for all the lost years of my own growing. At thirty-four my life should extend into far distant springs and summers of graduations and marriages, of autumn vacations in the mountains with tent and camp stove and oil lamp, to snowy winters, and grandchildren.

So many books unread, so much to know. I had wanted to go back to school, to get my master's degree, to teach, to write, to practice at the piano until I can play all of Bach's *Toccata and Fugue in D-Minor* without any mistakes.

There go the piano lessons, the ballet lessons, three years of orthodontics down the tubes. What a shame my folks wasted all that money having my teeth straightened. Now I'll have the straightest teeth in the cemetery.

I hate this self-pity. I have lately acquired the annoying habit of reading the obituaries in the newspaper first.

I think too much. I'm treading water as hard as I can and still going under. I want nothing more than to sit in the closet with the door shut and howl and curse in the dark. I want to go to bed and never get up again.

seven

I RECEIVED ANOTHER
letter from Jennifer. She writes:

> Believe it or not we just got your X-mas card. The
> U.S. mail service is wonderful — at 13¢ a throw.
>
> . . . we are finishing up the run of *That Championship
> Season* I directed. David did a fantastic set. Damn good
> in fact! Before that I played the lead "bod" in Pinter's
> *The Lovers*, a one-act with two people. It was bad and a
> bomb, but I was great! This time we have a well-
> balanced cast. Ensemble playing is terrific. I did it!
> Hot Damn! I find I have talent in another direction.
> The house looks like hell, but —
>
> Anyway, as you've no doubt observed from the sloppy
> handwriting — I'm feeling no pain. I think I've dis-
> covered the answer to my twice weekly drinking
> binges. Instead of getting drunk, or wringing my
> hands, calling long-distances, or making endless lists
> (oh, I make all kinds of lists, budgets, plans, etc.) I'll
> write you instead! As it happens we bought a lot of

stamps, so until they are gone you may get a bunch of dribble in the mail.

Dear, dear Jenny. She drinks too much. Jenny came to Hollywood at nineteen, a year older than I was. Her hair was red, her eyes dark brown, and her cheeks had dimples. I thought she was very beautiful. She thought her nose was too large. "It's my *father's* nose," she used to wail.

We shared a furnished apartment of horrid small rooms with orange furniture and dark prints of roses on the walls. Sometimes we talked all night long, whispered to each other things we had never told anyone else. And as we grew from children to women, the ties between us became stronger, the friendship mellowed.

"Life is a bitch," Jenny informed me when we first met, exercising at the ballet barre, sweating, stretching tight back and thigh muscles. "One . . . two . . . three . . . four. . ." She held her head high and kept her back very straight. "How old are you kid?" *Devant, en seconde, en arrière.*

Holding the barre, facing the mirror in fifth position: "I'm eighteen," I said.

"You look thirteen." *Demi-plié. Devant, en seconde, en arrière.*

"You look twenty-five." *Dégagé . . . développé.* She threw back her head in a fit of laughter.

"Life's a bitch," she said again.

We loved each other enormously from the start. Jenny took good care of me, offering sisterly advice. ("Heaven's sake Jody, fix yourself up a little bit, use some more make-up. Eye shadow. And don't wear *pink*. You look like Alice in Wonderland in pink.")

40

An actress should not look like Alice in Wonderland, I thought. Maybe I should do something about it. Cut my hair. Yes . . . and eye shadow. A charming ingenue! I should try for juveniles. Producers don't like to hire kids, so that's my best bet. *You look thirteen.* Purple, drawn carefully across the eyelid, that's it. Black liner. My eyebrows are all wrong. My head is too round. Purple up at the corner, that's it. . . . Oh, hell. All it looks like is I've got two black eyes! Wash it off again.

I leaned my arms on the edge of the washbasin, bent toward the mirror, waist-long hair swinging in my eyes. *Absurd.* Oh, shining flame hair. Titian locks. White teeth glistening through crimson lips. Skin like milk. Delicate arched brows, delicate purple shadows. *Not me.* The pain of innocence. Down the drain. Who chose me this face? *Genes and chromosomes. Sperm and ova.* Without any make-up I am invisible. I disappear.

"Jenny," I said. "Cut my hair."

She did.

"Oh," I said. "It looks like a broom!" Pale blond hair curled in long circles on the floor. I began to cry.

"I'm sorry," Jenny said. "I never said I could cut hair."

I climbed onto the bed, on my knees, holding the cut hair in my hands.

"I'm sorry, Jo. I really am. . . ." She touched my arm, and I pushed her away. She said, "But it's not too bad, is it? It won't crack the mirror."

Touch me. Don't touch me. No room, no room, shouted the Mad Hatter. Poor Alice.

Bits and pieces: a scrawled autograph from Sakini on the program cover of *Teahouse of the August Moon.* "To my personal Alice in Wonderland. My love and kisses for being so wonderful to work with. You will find your 'cricket'."

41

From another old program cover: *Holiday for Lovers.*
"All the best from here on to the top!"

Critque. February 6. Physical release and relaxation,
definitely needs more release. (Made good improvement
during rehearsal.)

May 1. Interesting vocal quality. Good stage standard.
Variety good. "Don't upstage yourself. Take off a few
pounds and you'll make a charming ingenue."

June 6. "You seem too reserved and aloof—afraid of
showing much emotion, yet under a lot of prodding you
show a nice warmth, humor, maturity, etc., which may
account for your giggles at times, eh? A bit slow on learning
lines, ok for stage, but I'd speed up for TV work."

August 13. "Excellent blending of part fancy and part
fact in the analysis of the character. Study use of body
movements, position, and gesture to obtain the best theat-
rical effect and gain the focus when it should be yours.
Enjoyed working with you again."

("You *glow* on stage," Jenny told me.)

Smile. The man from the photographers' is on the front
row for performance stills. *Smile.* There's an agent in the
audience tonight. *Smile.* I am doing Anya in *The Cherry
Orchard.* Jenny is off every day doing a film. She spends
hours in make-up, and then simply hangs around wearing
shorts and carrying a tennis racquet, waiting. *Smile.* But
watch out for that guy shooting the brassiere ad. He wants
more than a pretty picture.

"Are we going to sit around here like holes in the ground again this month?" I said.

A ring of blue smoke circled Jenny's head like a halo. "We could call the theatres again."

"I'm starving, and still I'm getting fat. My mother told me I should learn to be a secretary."

"You call this time. There's a whole new list in *Variety*."

"No open readings. Have your agent call us, dear."

"Here, the LeGrand. Did we call that one last time?" She showed me the number in the listing.

"Yes. No open readings."

"The Angel's Theatre. The guy I talked to last month said 'How old are you, dear?' I said 'Twenty-two.' He said 'Come on over, dear. I'll introduce you to the producer!'"

"We ought to go over," I said.

"He was probably the janitor!" Jenny hooted.

•   •   •   •

The summer before I knew Mark, I knew Paul. Successful (compared to everyone else I knew), he was a gifted actor with a knack for dueling — with rapiers or with words. Paul was older than I, proud, self-assured, and very sophisticated.

There was a time when duels were arranged to settle a point of honor, and young noblemen, meeting secretly in fields fought with swords and knives, and died on the spot. Now no one dies of it, though the sport continues in an amiable, indulgent sort of way.

The sounds of competition echoed off the vaulted ceiling and bare walls. The contestants wore white. Paul looked good in white.

"Outside high."

"Inside high."

Counting "hits"—five touches won a bout. Paul counter-parried the blade well. The German disengaged Paul's blade, passed the point into an open line by making a small movement around Paul's guard. He lunged.

"Touch." The bell and light recorded the hit.

"That's five."

Paul made a courteous salute to the German, a matter of form. "Nicely done," he said. He removed his glove, and then his mask. "How did I look?"

"You look like Ben Gazzara," I told him.

He tapped the point of the electric *epeé* with his thumb. "He was faster. I'll beat him in sabers, though." Paul liked to win.

He did. That made all the difference.

"Did it land?" Paul was exhuberant.

"Yes, touch." The first judge.

"Touch."

"Touch."

The German looked as if he were having a stroke, saluting in grudging admiration. Paul marched away without looking back. I thought he would have made an admirable Musketeer.

"Who are you this time," I said. "Athos, Porthos, Aramis, or D'Artagnan?"

Paul's smile faded.

"Why is it so important to win?" I asked.

"Winning is everything," he said.

Later, at his apartment, he got out a copy of his current script and pretended to read his lines. "I'm up for a big part first thing in the morning. I've got to make it great. Stay and give me some moral support, feed me lines. —I won't attack you right away, I promise. I'll keep one hand behind my back."

"Sure you will."

"Mmmm. You smell good." He kissed me on the neck.

"That's not me. That's my Windsong on your mind." I moved toward the door.

"Come on, relax. The coast is clear." Parry.

"No. I can't. It's late. I've got an early class." Riposte.

"You're already the greatest thing in show business since the immortal Duse did *Francesca da Rimini*. Come on, I'll keep both hands behind my back." Counterparry.

"I can't," I said.

"You know all the rules, don't you? All the thou-shalt-nots. Well, I've got news for you. Naïveté is the most exaggerated virtue in the world." Touch.

"I am not naïve."

"Like a lamb," he said softly.

Some for the glories of this world, and some
    sigh for the Prophet's Paradise to come;
Ah, take the cash, and let the credit go
    Nor heed the rumble of the distant drum!

Ah, make the most of what we yet may spend,
    Before we too into the Dust descend:
Dust into dust, and under dust to lie,
    Sans wine, sans song, sans singer, and sans—end

"Omar Khayyam," he said. He quoted Kant and Huxley too. But mostly, he quoted himself. "Life is short. We all end up in dirt. There is no plan, except whatever we make for ourselves. Right and wrong are nice, shadowy words. There is no God. Men make their own rules. Do you really believe I'm going to burn forever in somebody's fire if I say there is no God? Are you afraid I'll ruin your chances of salvation?"

I shrugged. Spirits dueled inside my head, half of them angels and the other half goat-footed beasts. I felt, with guilt, that Paul might be right. I thought of the good, bearded faces of the apostles in Sunday school books, of virgin angels with phosphorescent wings spread protectively over the children of earth. Saint Paul, Augustine, and Thomas Aquinas, fading like fairies, and no one left to clap them back to life. I belonged to a purer and simpler race of beings—outdated. Not of this world.

"Take the cash," Paul said, "and let the credit go. Have you ever been to Mexico?"

"No."

"It's a good experience for a proper, well-bred girl."

We tramped through a dozen florid Mexican shops and sidewalk stalls full of plaster bulls and velvet art. Christ was crucified on every corner, all red wounds and hideous agony. Street vendors offered tortillas, tripe soup, tacos (filled with what I was sure were chopped chicken feet), flavored ices and soft drinks. The sidewalks were full of street musicians, dancers, and exploding firecrackers.

"What are they celebrating?"

"Who knows? I'd say life. But probably not." A paper-mache figure of a skeleton, strung with fuses, exploded amid great hilarity. A cockfight in an alleyway shed blood and feathers into the uproar. The dying bird lay clawing at the spattered rocks, his talons furious even in death. Paul pushed his hands deep into his pockets, and his cigarette illuminated his eyes. "Sometime I'll show you a bullfight," he said. "Mankind at his best."

We had a little to drink. A slim bottle of tequila passed back and forth. I ate a little. Paul paid for the dinners and we walked in silence across the square. Paul whistled softly between his teeth, a soft hissing sound that was lost in sudden street noise.

We went to a room in a private house that belonged to a friend of his (out celebrating). Paul held my elbow as we went up a dark stairway. The door opened a crack.

"Where is the light?" I said.

He shut the door.

"Where is the light?"

He touched my cheek. "Jody. What are you thinking?"

"Hmmm. What do you want me to say?" I felt too warm, and a little dizzy.

"I believe people should always say whatever they're thinking."

"Didn't Thomas Edison ever make it this far south?"

He lit a candle. He whispered to me, I felt his breath in my ear. "Hmmm," I said again. "I think you're a dirty old man."

A celebration of life. Pity us all that we must die, and loathsome caverns devour us—all the beautiful people who must wrinkle and rot in a celebration of life.

I was two people, one an actor, the other an observer, critical, watching, seeing the two of us, however vague and confused. I saw myself moving with a slow but inevitable gravitation. *Where now?* Soft Mexican music of Piteros players passed below the window, rippling into the room, the liquid melody of the flutes and the gentle steady drumbeat a delicate, flowing inundation. Where now? The play seemed frozen in a picture that finally began to move with jerks of light, like an old-time film.

Leonard Lust crushed the slender, yielding form of Gloria Goodbody to his broad chest. "I've loved you since the day I

47

saved you from the iron clutches of that scoundrel, Diamond Dick."

He leaned rapturously toward her and their lips met in sweet and tender ecstasy. "Darling Leonard," she gasped. "Oh, you dear, foolish boy, why didn't you speak sooner and I should never have run away with Diamond Dick!"

Their adoring eyes met. "What are an old man's diamonds," said she (her eyes were wet with tears and her lips trembled), "compared to a young man's love?"

And she was clasped to his manly bosom for one long Eternal Moment.

Shades, I thought. A silent movie. "But it's only eight-thirty."

Paul's mouth followed his moving hands. "That doesn't matter. Now does it?"

I guessed not. "I guess you win," I said.

"Touché," he said.

I half-expected that out of a peal of thunder a deep Voice would announce, "This is God. Shame on you." None did. Show me. Make me feel *something.* In all my life I've never felt one thing—not anger or hate or love, or even passion. Touch me. Show me how. *Now.*

"I hope I didn't take advantage of you," Paul said.

"You didn't. I wasn't that drunk."

"But this wasn't your first time." He half-smiled, raised on one elbow. "And I wanted to be the first."

All the blurred liquid softness of it was gone. I felt a great urge to run, like a person on fire. "You were."

He shook his head doubtfully. "You're not the lamb I thought you were."

I gathered up my clothes. "Now, don't be mad," he said. "And don't get lost. The bathroom's that way."

48

I didn't want to be lost. Not in any way. One minute I was small and cold and naked in a strange bathroom, and the next I was at the bottom of the stairs, alone.

"Wait—you can't go home alone." The stairs creaked. "Who knows what evil lurks at every corner!" Paul dropped his hands from the bannister into his pockets. He whistled again. The sound was a whisper almost too soft to hear.

What is love, Mama? Not this. No, not this.

A little after four A.M.—

"So? How was it? What did you do?" Jenny asked, not opening her eyes.

"Nothing. We ate. And we saw a very old movie." I stopped carefully, not looking at her.

Jenny opened one eye toward the clock. "Did you sleep with Paul?"

"We didn't sleep," I said.

•   •   •   •

Shakespeare 138: King Lear—an introductory lecture on the glories of classical theatre. I sit amid a stack of books, shifting in my chair, fidgeting with my pencil.

"The exploration of an amoral universe. Deliberately pre-Christian. Notice how Lear prays to Jupiter. It's the idea of Greek philosophy. The language is all important." The director's skin was so loose even his fingers were webbed. He clipped together several sheets of paper. *Time.* Mother's darling he used to be, with skin as tight and rosy as a berry.

He peered at the papers in his duckyfoot fingers.

Babyfingers. What if there is a *baby*? Soft and smelling sweet. *A kiss is the unborn knocking at the door.* Who said that? The unborn born unborn born unborn. Moving in the womb. Mine. My baby. I'd be a bad mother. Bluejeans and dirty tennis shoes. Bone of my bone. Flesh. Open to me my love, my dove, my undefiled. I couldn't resist so much flattery. No one ever told me I was beautiful before. Where other boys brought flower corsages to their dates, mine brought a sack of potatoes, and once, a cheese. Thou art fair, my love; thou hast doves' eyes . . . thy lips are like a thread of scarlet, thy two breasts are twins which feed among the lilies. Blessed are those who love in Holy Matrimony. Hole-y. No such word. Milk and honey are under thy tongue. The Emancipation of Emotion. Definitely needs more physical release. (Made good improvement though, yes?) Ten-fifteen.

"Not Roman then?" someone says.

"Well, now you could say Roman from the Greek. Evidently Shakespeare was not very well acquainted with the old English gods."

Polite laughter. The director unwound the paperclip slowly and curled it between his palms.

Let's explore madness to find sanity. Rorshach. Freud. The Undiscovered Self. The Intensity of Suffering. Suffering is amoral moral immoral. Choose one. Moving unborn born unborn.

Oh, Jumping Jupiter. Pray for us all now and in the hour of our un-hole-y emancipation.

"Then," says the old man, "is mortality significant, or a game of pranks played on us?"

Open to me my love, my dove. It was *not* last *night* but the *night* be*fore, twenty*-four *rob*bers came *knocking* at my *door.* They have pills and things, Paul said. The unborn.

You don't have to worry about that you don't have to. A pill a day. The Rhetorical Question. The Rhetorical Answer.

The paperclip falls to the floor, and the director stoops to retrieve it. Perhaps he will shed his old skin like a snake and grow some new. There is a ring on his finger. Somebody loves him I wonder who I wonder who it can be?

Ten-twenty.

Tick tock tick tock.

Ten-thirty.

Poor Alice.

I am doing Strindberg's *Miss Julie,* "battling with heaven and hell." Someone in the cast has discovered she is pregnant. They told her quinine would abort the baby, so she has drunk enough of it to cause her to be terribly sick. She lies on the cold dressing room floor, her knees drawn up to her chest, in great pain. Someone else suggests a coat hanger.

The baby's father has taken another lover, a young man this time, the star of a television "soap," and he can no longer be bothered with her problems.

I spend an hour a day at the ballet barre (not enough time.) I hurt every place. I was not meant to be a ballerina. I am too small. The mirrors embarrass me. There are no mirrors onstage.

Jennifer said, "I went to a strange party last night. Every one was blowing grass. The men hung together and the girls hung together. I got this feeling that the men were with the men and the girls were with the girls because they *preferred* it that way. Anyway, I felt out of place and was ready to leave when I saw Paul, and suddenly he was telling

51

about his love life. He's living with a black girl and a man. Before I left, Paul reached out and kissed the man on the mouth. Then several of the other guys came in and hugged him goodnight and made flirting remarks—I heard them. Paul flirted right back. I was shocked, but I didn't let on to him. He thinks it's quite normal. All his friends do it. He doesn't care. He only wants sex in any form. He says he still loves you, but what he has going now is what he needs. He thinks you two could still make a go of it. He didn't tell me not to tell you."

Bastard. In the immortal words of Mr. Whitesides, "I may vomit."

Maybe that's the reason for the cancer. Justice. Retribution. Punishment. Who knows? Maybe if I had behaved better then . . . had been less—willful, less stubborn. Maybe if I had stayed home and become a secretary.

This is absurd, I tell myself now, to worry over things that happened such a long time ago. I recognize that I am, or have been, good *and* bad, not good *or* bad.

But *everything happens for a reason.* Basic physics. Cause and effect. The mind grasps at answers, seeks reasons where there are none. Why do I need to believe there is a reason? Does it matter?

It would have happened anyway, I tell myself. It would have happened anyway.

Would it?

It matters!

Mark is an idealist, a dreamer with the soul of a poet. I think of our time together as bonfires at the beach, waterfront carnival lights reflected in the water, seen from the top basket of the ferris wheel. He was folk songs on his guitar, and collections of sea-shells. He was long walks out to the end of the pier where little boys and old men threw crayfish bait on fishing lines out into the waves, and he was the shrill cries of seagulls. I knew what his favorite color was and he thought I was a "fairy princess." *Was?* We sat in our shallow sandstone cave and looked out at the ocean. We ate tuna fish sandwiches, and Mark wrote I LOVE YOU on the brown lunch bag and hid it in a hole in the rocks. (Sometime, in fifty years or so, we'll go back, a little wrinkled, white-haired lady and gentleman, holding hands, to see if it is still there.) *Will we?* Our bodies were covered with sand and salt. We laughed and were happy and alone in the world. I never said "I love you" to anyone else.

• • • •

*Our footsteps cross the shifting wind
where sandpipers dance down the shore.
You buy bananas-on-a-stick
that taste of salt or tears, before
we lie upon that glimmering bed
below the cliffs where tides have left
shells like wet, white bones, and sleep
christcrossed where sky and earth are cleft
      by sea and froth.*

*Your lips taste salt like creatures born
of green sea-water; if you bleed
pale drops the color of the sea
will fall into the ebbing sand.*

We please ourselves deliciously,
we're satisfied, and glad of life.
The world will end this way, won't it?
It will, without a doubt, and at
                    the speed of light.

•   •   •   •

I always wanted to write, or paint, or something. To be
an actress and live other people's lives. It always seemed
that people in books and plays lived as life ought to be, vital
and passionate and beautiful. I never could until I met Mark,
and then I began to protest spending the last few years of
my life being someone not myself.

Beloved Mark—did he see where I was going? I was
drowning and he threw out a rope. He was so good. "I can't
even cook," I admitted. "But maybe I'll get better."

While I toured, I wrote him copious letters.

Hello from one of the Dirty Dozen and Their Traveling
Tenement! We're going to write Sleaze, Inc. on the side of
the trailer. Our trash bags are overflowing with old show
programs, candy wrappers, banana skins, etc. More mos-
quitos. It's raining again. We're thinking of calling ourselves The Jolly Consumptives. Cough, cough.

•   •   •   •

We drove to Bowman, North Dakota last night. Up at
seven and drive most of the night. Then we'll be in

Winnipeg tomorrow. Are you still following me on the map? I love it!

• • • •

Spent last night in a hotel in Muskegon. The water wouldn't run out of the sink, and the plug in the bathtub didn't fit. I had to plug up the hole with my heel to keep the water in. Somebody's baby cried all night and a drunk talked to himself for hours outside our door. Yucch.

• • • •

Did you know I'm insured by Lloyd's of London?

• • • •

Chicago—we have a necklace of dandelions hanging from the rear-view mirror. Yesterday I met a little girl who was overcome by standing next to a *real actress*! She said, "Gee, can I touch you?" She said she thought I was the "prettiest one" in the show. I could really get to like this. Lots of kids and old ladies ask us for autographs.

• • • •

I feel—something I can't find words for. Like time is so

short and things go by so quickly, and that frightens me.

• • • •

I dreamed last night I was in a concentration camp. We all
had guns and were running along close to the walls. There
was a door, and we all rushed in, and then just waited
quietly for them to come in and get us. Then I was burying
something, and an old man came by. He said, "How old are
you, thirteen or fourteen?" I was insulted, so I did a little
tap dance and said, "I'm twenty-one, and I'd vote in the
next election, only I'm not registered."

• • • •

Tonight we play a huge old barn of a building. I can hardly
see the back wall from the stage. They've got eight baskets
of flowers up there. If they don't move them we'll all be
hidden in the foliage. We went through Minneapolis and
St. Paul early this morning. Can't remember much, but
neither can I remember sleeping—just being tired and
uncomfortable, and having my leg or my hand or arm go
numb at close intervals.

• • • •

There was so much I wanted to tell you, but I'm too tired.
About New York City. About midnight rehearsals in hotel
rooms. About all the company jokes (mostly dirty). About

being so tired you think you're going to be verrry sick. And all about the beautiful people I've met. . . .

. . . .

One of the guys gave me a bouquet of scaggy wildflowers and a real hawkfeather to brighten up the otherwise drab hotel room. He found sombody's falsie as we were about to leave Chicago, and he was embarrassed to ask who it belonged to. "Nobody would admit it if it was theirs anyway," he said. It didn't belong to me!

. . . .

Chew Mail Pouch Tobacco, Treat yourself to the Best. If daisies are . . . your favorite flower . . . keep pushing up . . . those miles per hour . . . Burma Shave. Kokomo. 14 miles. Eat. Budweiser, King of Beers. 4:24 P.M.

. . . .

Hope I don't have to be nice to anybody tonight. Hope they just leave me alone. I get so tired of being nice to people, saying the same things, over and over. I'll be glad to get home. We'll have taquitos on Olvera Street.

. . . .

Mark replied:

Looking forward to having "Taquitos for Two," (new song I just wrote.) Sorry this is such a short letter, but you must remember I am a short man. Although I am an intellectual giant.

. . . .

I sent him one last letter from the road.

I miss you so much I could go out and eat worms. But you know how I hate to eat alone.

Sometime I'll tell you a parable about the Sisty Ugler and the Prince. I never saw you as anyone but the Prince. Never the troll. You have been slaying dragons for me. You'll never understand how big and how terrible some of my dragons are. They were growing fat from being fed by other people. I used to hate myself most of the time. Now I like myself again. I don't want you to misunderstand. Mark, I have done things I felt I should be sorry about, but never truly was until now. . . .

"I wish you hadn't told me," he said.

I wish I hadn't too. Oh how I do wish it! But I thought he might know, might somehow be able to tell. I meant only to be honest, not to hurt him. He put his fist through the wall and brought back bloodied knuckles, and nothing more was ever said. He loved me anyway.

But the fairy princess was forever dead.

A few days later there was a note from Jenny saying she rented a cottage near the beach for a couple of days but she wasn't going to be there and I was free to stay.

The beach at night is full of quiet dark birds and white waves. I was glad to be there. Maybe things would all come together again. I sunned, and rested, and read. Tomorrow, I thought, I'll call Mark.

That night I called Paul.

"It's been a long time, Love," he said. We had not talked for nearly a year. "I'll bring along a bottle of Cabernet Sauvignon."

"Am I worth that?"

"A good wine never hurts."

"I don't want to drink," I said. "Don't bother."

"It's no bother," he said.

"I really don't want to drink."

"What do you want?" He paused. "You know, you're treating me like a brother you haven't seen for a long time."

"Maybe I'm a little nervous," I said, my voice quavering.

"Whatever," he said. "Give me twenty minutes."

Now why did I do that? Oh, my dear sweet, gentle Mark. That's *why*. Take the cash. I will not do this, I won't.

I locked the door and turned out the lights. The cottage was hard to find in daylight—Paul would never find it in darkness.

This is insane, I thought, sitting in the dark. He's not coming to murder me. He's not even bringing the Cabernet Sauvignon. The soft motor of a car whirred along the highway. I held my breath. I'd leave it to chance. If Paul found the cottage in the dark I'd let him in. Open to me. If he couldn't find it—that's the breaks.

Take the cash. Don't think about that. Think about something else. Mama. The old organ at home, and Mama playing "Jesu, Joy of Man's Desiring," *semplice e grazioso*:

> Word of God, our flesh that fashioned
> with the fire of faith impassioned. . . .

I think of a round paperweight Mama kept—a glass ball filled with plastic snow. The low notes shook the snow, shook the little bones in my ears, vibrated my teeth. The snow settled all around the little house. The notes fade, the words remain.

It's so hard not to remember, not to think, not to think—(a closeup of Paul's hands moving softly across damp skin. His mouth.) I felt an actual physical pain, an ache beyond laughing or crying, at the impossibility of this scene. *Cannibals*. ("Is it white wine, or red," said one cannibal to the other, "with Presbyterians?") I am no cannibal. Who am I, Mark? Remembered. Who-I-Am. *Not this*.

The car cruised by several times, missing the dark driveway each time. I exhaled a soft typhoon that ended in a hiccup.

After a few minutes the phone rang as I knew it would. And rang. And rang again. I never answered. After awhile the pain and the hiccups faded.

That night, if the angels cheered, I cried myself to sleep.

•　　•　　•　　•

They played the *Brandenburg Concertos* when Mark and I were married. Jenny (married first, to a tall, balding artist from San Francisco) flew in from an engagement as a Las Vegas showgirl to be my matron of honor. She would have preferred Bacharach to Bach, but she endured.

I invited Paul. (There. Do you see? Look, I have survived. Look, I am happier than I ever was! Do you see?)

"Hey," he said. "You look great."

I smiled knowing I looked terrific! *Goodbye, Alice.*

Among the wedding gifts were Paul's, two expensive goose-down pillows with a note attached: "For Remembrance, Paul." I crumpled the note and tossed it at the nearest wastebasket. (There's rosemary, that's for remembrance; pray, love, remember: and there is pansies, that's for thoughts. There's fennel for you, and columbines, and rue. O, you must wear your rue with a difference . . . *for bonny sweet Mark is all my joy.*)

•   •   •   •

So much for fairy tales. People have no right, in the name of love, or honesty, to cause pain to one another. I am who I am now. It is today that counts, this moment, and whatever tomorrow might be. The rest is over and done with.

My heart keeps time with the ticking clock on the wall. Time. *A catalectic tetrameter of iambs marching.* James Joyce said that. Or wrote it anyway. Time. We never will be so young again.

Point of View

I am stronger
   than
I am fragile
   and far

too far away
 from
innocence
 I am
(having lost
 it all
between one
 abyss
and the next
 without
undue remorse
 or even
acid indigestion)
 now
to wonder how
 I walked
a double line
 the
emerging woman
 less
rebellious
 than
the girl.

eight

MY HAIR DIDN'T ALL FALL
out. (I'm so glad!). New hair is growing—it sticks out all
over my head, and much of it is white. I look like a
dandelion.

The boys planted radish seeds today, tiny dark seeds that
will become—or so said the package—"bright scarlet radishes of globe shape and superb quality." Plant early, sow
thinly. It's probably too early. The snow has barely cleared.
It's muddy out.

Happy Valentine's Day! It rained ice today. I stood out
in the cold and wet for a long time, letting the water freeze
on my face, waving my arms and blowing out clouds of
warm fog.

Then, inside, I sat at the window for a long time,
watching the wind blow waves of sleet across the road. It
was a super storm, loud and flashy, the kind that lays ice on

telephone wires and turns tree limbs to crystal. The boys sat on my lap, all of us warm and quiet together, until it was too dark to see.

Something happened then. A high, better than any drug-induced high, a feeling that almost burst my mind apart. I can't find a name for it, that feeling of intense awareness and content. What a joy it is to be alive! To feel and see, to smell, to hear, to touch, to experience and love—all wonderful, miracle things! It was the whole yard suddenly made perfect in the rain, the fence posts and the mail box, and the root-born crack in the sidewalk at once magnified, the hum of the wind in the wires, the radish seeds under the frozen mud, the pink half-moons under the fingernails, the steady in-and-out flow of breath, all enhanced with a piercingly beautiful—almost saccharin—awareness of symmetry and timelessness.

There is a painting of Christ on a mountaintop called *The Transfiguration*. He and three of His disciples, seeing beyond His death, "and His face did shine as the sun. . . and Jesus came and touched them and said, 'Arise, and be not afraid.'"

Be not afraid!

Today there will be a celebration. Today I breathe air that first blew as a fierce wind out of the arctic, over icebergs, across seal rookeries, over the salty Pacific, past the Golden Gate, above the giant Sequoias and across the granite Sierras to me.

It is a matter of fact that this wind carries with it a kind of immortality: *argon atoms* that exist continually in the atmosphere. They do not perish, they do not change. They remain. With each breath I inhale forty million billion argon atoms and exhale them unchanged into the atmosphere, where they are scattered like seeds on the wind. Some of those same argon atoms that swirled in the primeval lungs of the first Devonian fish to slither out of salt-water onto shore will be in my next breath, and those same atoms I exhale will be part of the birth gasp of infants born a thousand years away.

I see a circularity, an almost mystical bond between the distant past and the remote future. And if it is true that we are one with the dinosaur and the dodo bird, we are also one with Christ and Michaelangelo, with Mozart and Shakespeare and Thomas Paine. I am not alone in this, nor is anyone. And this is something to celebrate!

What is such a moment worth? What would I give for another brief moment like this, so precious, so perishable? I feel as though my vision has been extended. To *love* is enough. To *be* loved is enough.

We made paper hearts and snowflakes and hung them in the window.

"Hey, something's wrong with my shirt," Remy says, concerned. He wears his pajama shirt wrong-side-out. The picture and lettering on the front are reversed, and what said TRANS AM last night, tonight says MA SNART.

"Ma Snart?" he says between laughing fits. "My shirt says Ma Snart?"

He laughs and rolls around on the floor. I laugh with him. Great reservoirs of laughter spill and cascade and deluge us. Together we roll on the floor, roaring so hard our ribs ache. I can't stop laughing. Then comes a flooding of tears—not of sorrow, but a cleansing, a kind of cathartic. I crawl to my knees, gasping for breath. "Oh. Oh, my!" I pull him to me and hug him hard. "Oh, my. You cuckoo clock! Oh, you old cuckoo clock! How I love you!"

I can laugh out loud again. Somehow the anesthetic has worn off. I can laugh *out loud.*

Do not spoil
  with clumsy hands
this delicate almost-crystal
                    world.

Today
  no thunder trembles me,
  no earthquake rocks my
                  applecart.

And if
  I take another breath—
  just one breath

              more,

surely
  I shall burst
  and silently, magnificently
                  soar!

·   ·   ·   ·

   The boys' radishes are coming up. I smell the greening of
the earth, I am more intensely aware of sound and color and
the passing of time than I ever was before. I find time to
listen to Christopher's four-year-old chatter, to draw with
him, and paint (like Dylan Thomas, we paint the sky and
grass and trees any color we choose). I find time purely to
enjoy. I've listened to the *Brandenburg Concertos*, to Vivaldi,
and Telemann, and Scarlatti Masses. I read to the boys. I tell
them every day how very much I love them. I have even

found time to practice the piano. *Time*. Time is everything. Lord, don't let me waste time.

．　　．　　．　　．

At variables. Emotional highs followed by lows, like a weather chart.

I go to see the doctor with a painful right knee. He orders X-rays of the knee and blood tests, which show nothing abnormal, except that the white count is up and the sed rate is high. What does that mean? He writes, "Melanoma— possibility of metastasis" on the insurance papers. My heart skips a beat, and I wonder if it will start again. Has the "possibility of metastasis" not occurred to me? Of course it has. It occurs to me every time I cough, or hurt with the flu, or have a headache. I suffer acute anxiety attacks at the prospect of a simple office call.

I pretend it doesn't really hurt.

But it does. *It*. Hurts.

I am so-oo-ooo sick. I can't get out of bed without throwing up. I try to smile when Mark asks me if I feel well.

"Sure," I smile, and clench my teeth, and swallow hard. Why don't I just tell him the truth?—Because I'm still pretending, I'm scared.

．　　．　　．　　．

I can't pretend anymore. I am so tired. I throw up all day long and half the night. It's not getting better. I'll call Doctor Sontag tomorrow. It's one thing to be scared. It's another to be stupid.

I am *pregnant*.

"Is that possible?" I ask the nurse. Ninny. She looks at me as though I think I am, perhaps, the Virgin Mary.

"Have you been exposed?" she asks, as if it were a case of chicken pox. "If you've been exposed, then it's possible."

How can I be *pregnant*? "You're sure there is no mistake?"

"No mistake." She shakes her head.

How far along? I sink into the nearest chair, making a number of rapid calculations in my head. I have been meticulously careful. *Except once.* (Like an echo: "I missed you," I can hear Mark say. He traces a trail with his fingertip down my ribs. "You don't waste time, do you?" I say. "There's plenty of time.") It is possible.

I think of all the X-rays taken without a shield, the radioactive dyes, the liver scan, all the things done behind heavy doors marked CAUTION, and NUCLEAR MEDI-CINE, of all the drugs and anaesthetics. How far? . . . almost *four months*. Oh, my God. How could I not know? My head is like a helium balloon floating inches off my body.

"When was your last menstrual period?" the nurse asks. "Mrs. Harper?—Are you all right?"

"I'm fine." My head returns. "I don't know. I haven't . . . it's been months. Doctor Sontag said it was the illness, that it would take a while for things to get back to normal."

"I see."

"Pregnancy . . . is dangerous, isn't it?"

"There are indications that pregnancy will activate

cancer," she says.

Doctor Sontag estimates 16 weeks. I figure 13 or 14 at the most.

"*What to do about a pregnancy?*" The doctor shakes his head and taps a pencil on the edge of his desk. "Many doctors would advise a termination, but there is little evidence to support this view. There are studies available which indicate that the outcome of cancer in pregnant women is not different from that in non-pregnant women. Other studies show estrogen levels of pregnancy speed up the growth of malignant cells."

Fifty-fifty. A drawn game.

Knowing how this pregnancy may increase the chance of recurrence of the cancer, all the old dragons have returned. Mark says he had nothing to do with it, that it's something I caught in the hospital from a dirty needle. Ha, ha. I am sick and cross. I yell and complain a lot, and then I feel guilty afterward because I have wasted valuable time in anger and frustration.

Abortion is out of the question. I can't even consider that possibility. I am aware of the dangers of radiation and drugs to the fetus. Doctor Sontag emphasized the possibility of impairment.

It's cold out tonight—very cold. Mark is unusually quiet while he gets ready for bed. He lies next to me, turning to kiss me, and his whole body touches mine. I turn over on my side, away from him, facing the wall. He lifts himself up just enough to arrange the covers over and around me. "Goodnight," he says to my back.

"Mark," I whisper. "I am so afraid." I am trapped again. There's nowhere to go. Just a wall.

"Go ahead and cry." Mark brushes his thumb gently across my cheek.

"I can't cry. There aren't even any tears."

In the middle of the night I wake to find myself praying. And I find there are still tears. *"Oh, let it be all right, please. Please, please let it be all right."*

•   •   •   •

At variables again. Yesterday was a downer. Today I am up.

I choose to live if I still have a choice. I *choose* to let this baby live. At any rate, I have the power to direct my life while it is mine—whether it be for six months or sixty years more.

•   •   •   •

Today I am thirty-five. I felt the baby move. He is eight inches long, he weighs six ounces. His heart pumps twenty-five quarts of blood a day. What a beautiful thing to happen on my birthday.

I read today about the metamorphosis of a Cecropia moth. The lilacs are blooming, purple and white. The earth smells of things that have withered and gone to seed and bloom again. The scent of the flowers is incredible. The boys brought me a small armful for a vase in the kitchen, but I can smell them everywhere. I heard a Swedish proverb: Fear less, hope more; talk less, say more; sit less, walk more; eat less, chew more; whine less, breathe more; hate less, love more; and all good things are yours.

I need something to keep my mind busy. I've decided to write again. I must be able to unearth something of value to someone—to sow where others may reap, so to speak.

If I had one thought to give my children—a legacy of sorts—it would be this, and it should be graven with an iron pen on rock forever: make every day count. Just that. *Make every day count.* The race is not always to the swift.

nine

WHEN I WAS SIX I USED TO
lie in bed beside my cousin Ginger, who was ten. Ginger
could pop her chewing gum gloriously loud in the dark. I
envied her that. I thought if only I could learn to pop my
gum like that I would be happy forever. Now that I am able
to lie in bed and pop my gum with a genuine garish
abandon, I find that it does not necessarily bring everlasting
happiness.

What it does is make Mark mad. "Will you cut that
out?" he snaps. He is peevish and annoyed, trying to study
for an archeology exam.

I tuck the gum under my tongue. Everlasting happiness
is something else.

Maybe a warm typewriter. I work very hard at it,
sometimes I work late into the night. Tomorrow is tenuous.
Today is quicksilver. I am ravenous. I devour T. S. Eliot and
Theodore Roethke. When I am alone, I write. It must be
something hard, something challenging enough to wrench

my mind away from the insolvable crazies that frequent every day. I try, with dubious results, the disciplines of Shakespearean and Italian sonnets, and villanelles. I dream in iambic pentameter. I love writing, as I love theatre and ballet, and making love, and eating chocolate bars. I write four days a week. The fifth day I teach a creative writing workshop for the community school's adult education program. I don't know exactly how I fell into this, but it's nice. Saturday I clean up the house (which by nightfall is no longer clean and stays that way for the next six days).

How difficult it is to bring life to a piece of blank paper, to derive color and sound and movement and feeling from written words. The main thing is to continue writing.

I have sold several poems and some articles, so it must not be all bad. One editor writes that I may have been "too much influenced by the poetry of Dylan Thomas or some of the later surrealists," saying, "thus the language, just when it is supposed to surprise us most, takes rather predictable turns. Nevertheless, the poems are effective and one can hope for true originality from someone who can write of Neptune: 'If you bleed/Pale drops the color of the sea/Will fall into the ebbing sand.'"

Another writes, "A bit too inebriated with the sound, rather than sense, of words, but there are worse faults. A little more maturing should do wonders. . . ."

Maybe by the time I'm seventy or eighty I'll be quite mature. I should live so long.

In my head, in reading and writing, I escape what threatens me, whether it be dragons or dirty dishes. I am a master at the Ultimate Escape. When Bermuda is not far enough, when even La Cote d'Azure is too close for comfort, I try the orbits of Sirius A and Sirius B, or the Smoke Ring Nebula in the constellation of Lyrae, counting light years between swarms of galaxies, between Australopithecinae and Deity. I want to write thick volumes of the poetry of space and time, of huge things like meteors and nebulae, and of infinitely small things—whatever unimaginables whirl in the heart of an electron. I have developed a mania for science fiction, like some pimply-faced adolescent.

The room I write in is filled with books, mostly poetry, but lots of SF, too. Mark bought me a desk and a new typewriter. I have a pencil-holder Remy made, an orange juice can decorated with blue yarn and yellow construction paper. Thoreau's *Walden*, Whitman's *Leaves of Grass*, and the *Collected Poems of Dylan Thomas*, books by Ray Bradbury and Issac Asimov, Harlan Ellison and Kurt Vonnegut lie in comfortable disarray beside the empty skull of a horse we found baking in the Arizona sun one summer.

I want to know the nature of light, and electricity, and black holes. I want to figure out the great WHY of everything. There is not enough time to know enough. I don't want to die—so very much I don't want to die.

If I were given a choice of how long I might live with my immediate mental and physical equipment, I would certainly decide on a good deal longer than the three score and ten alloted. Or less. I like to think of people as the Tralfamadorians in Kurt Vonnegut's *Slaughterhouse Five* saw them—as continuous beings, not unlike long caterpillars, with fat baby's legs at one end and long, ancient legs at the other—beings forever all-one-piece, integrated and entire.

I'd like that.

ten

A LINE OF POETRY RUNS
through my head. Fearing to lose it if I do not write it
immediately, I try desperately to find a pencil and paper.
There are none to be found. I finally find two stubs, and
neither of them has a point. At last, a ballpoint pen! It is
dry. I make do with an orange crayon on the back of a gas
bill, writing: *A darkness in the weather of the eye.*

A nice line. Is it mine, or somebody else's? I hope it is
mine. Who knows?

I am becoming more noticeably pregnant. I look like one
of those fat Mesopotamian fertility goddesses. *The Venus of
Willendorf.* Mother Earth. The baby now has hair, eyebrows, eyelashes, and weighs about two pounds. I've heard
his heart beating. Maybe I will make a musician of him. I
clap the stereo-earphones around my belly and wake him
with Milhaud's *La Creation du Monde.* Whatever prophetic

messages the music contains are transmitted to him with the sound of my heartbeat. He hears, dancing a lively watery pre-natal ballet to the rhythms. Maybe he will be a dancer.

My mother is astounded and appalled that I am pregnant. She must think I never get out of bed.

Jennifer writes again. She scolds me.

How could you get pregnant again! And how *could* you possibly consider having this baby if you think it might make the cancer worse?

She doesn't understand that I *must choose* to have this child.

My drinking is still a problem to me, not, apparently to anyone else, because I don't do it that often (two times a week, an acceptable level, I guess.)

Anyway, I'm sorry for calling you when I've been drinking. But I truly am working on it—as well as on religion, diet, career,—and oh, yes, smoking. Hey! Hey! I want you to know I have quit smoking *except* when I'm drinking! At least, by Damn, I keep working on my imperfections.

I really don't know, for sure, what is real and what is necessary for survival. We kid ourselves so often, trying to make a 'meaningful' experience out of everything. It is possible some things have no meaning.

Jenny said once, "It's so *hard* to keep appreciating what you have, day to day. But there are very few things that cannot be overcome by a strong-willed person."

Death is one. In the dreamless times between dark and dawn, in the quiet nights of ticking clocks it comes to us, and we can't be indifferent. It *is* possible some things have no meaning. But I keep trying to find one.

I have decided to write a book. (Hasn't everybody!) I hope it will not require an editor's gentle postscript telling of the valiant (though unsuccessful) battle I waged against the Dark Forces of Fate.

I understand what I want to do—I feel it—a rediscovery of sensation after numbness, a sort of re-awakening. I want to assert my reality with an intensity others will recognize. I feel things I've never felt before. People are more beautiful than they were. Breath is sweeter. Colors are brighter. I live for today, and forget about yesterday and tomorrow. It gets easier.

It's not easy to write how it feels to be *alive*. It's an immeasurable thing. But I spend a lot of time measuring anyway. I change the baby's diaper, and fix a bottle for his nap, then I open a can of Coca Cola and turn on the radio, which plays a Beethoven Sonata, and I begin: "Monday morning. Out in the early-morning traffic, the fox-hunting, deer-stalking, big-game traffic. It must have reached 90 degrees already."

Now, what kind of a dumb beginning is that?

Sometimes we can write things we can't say out loud. In her epilogue to *Death Be Not Proud*, Frances Gunther wrote: "What a Joy life is! Why does no one talk about the Joy of Life?" That's what I'd like to do. Write about the Joy of Life.

"Joy is a fundamental emotion," wrote Dr. John Schindler. "Fundamental emotions exist as a continual background. Fundamental emotions have the greatest influence because they are constant and basic—regardless of what the superficial emotions are."

I find, barely into this book, that it is infinitely more trying than I thought it would be. I try to think about continuity and sequence, and steady progression toward a goal. I find myself so wound-up, so emotionally entangled in the work that, while my intentions are to magnify the Joy of Life, I find myself extremely nervous, short-tempered with my children and impossible to live with.

I think I should write what I know, so of course I will write about Jennifer. Although our lives have taken different directions she is as much a part of me as my heart. Jenny understands pain and escape. My scar is still tender, it still hurts a little. Jenny's scars, of a different nature, are tender, too. I wish we had talked long ago about living and dying. But we were too young. We talked about *Variety* and agents, Stanislavsky and "The Method," and whether Katherine Hepburn was truly great.

When we are young we never notice things until after they are gone.

("Wow!" she says. "Quote from me? Of course—you can use anything you want, if it will help. We theatre folks have BIG egos.

"You really opened a can of worms this time. David and I survive by not remembering the past, but for you, we'll try. You have such a gift. Hell, I knew it way back, and you did, too. The time just wasn't right.")

Well, Jenny, the time is right.

eleven

JENNY MARRIED DAVID in the second year of our friendship. She flew home from California to Ohio for the wedding, and wrote:

Dearest Jody,

I made it! Home all safe and sound. The flight was terrific—I spent this week visiting relatives and planning for the wedding. The bridesmaids' dresses are silk and turquoise. My dress isn't in yet. But they assure me it will be here in time. It is so beautiful!

I miss David something terrible. We write every day, but that doesn't help much. The cats are fine. They are getting better about "poo-pooing" on the floor. It should be a riot coming across country with them in the Volkswagen.

Gee, it's fun to get married and get presents—I'm really getting excited now, it is less than two weeks away. Help! Maybe I'd better read some more books first. Oh well, learning by doing is fun, too!

Dearest Jody,

You know how it is with us old married women, never enough time to write, what with working, cleaning, ironing, etc. . . . .

I have two words for you. GET MARRIED! It's great. The wedding was beautiful. Niagara was beautiful—only stayed there a day. We got to Provincetown the next day. We go to the beach on all sunny days. There haven't been many.

The cats are getting big and independent. The other day Putt-Putt went for a walk and didn't come back. We were miserable for three days. Some little boy found him in the middle of town. Now both cats have a lot of fleas.

David has been wonderful and I love him more every day.

This last month has been so hectic. We left P'town and went to New York and saw *West Side Story* and *Look Back in Anger*. Also went to a lot of art galleries.

Still have our cake—the top layer. I can't bear to eat it.

•　•　•　•

News of the Day Department: I weigh too much. I am bored and slowly going crazy. However, I am still madly in love with David, which is rather convenient since we live together.

Baby Department: Still none.

Money Department: Still none. Low on funds, due to rash spending, such as $2.98 for a shoe rack.

Career Department: David is painting up a storm.

We put "The Old Man with the Ice Wagon" in the art show—all the other artists entered bowls of fruit and landscapes. David heard a lot of favorable comments, so we cheered up a bit. He's made some jewelry. We go tomorrow to see a man about casting some of it.

Miscellaneous Department: I am reading *Candide*, by Voltaire, *The Idiot*, by Dostoyevsky, *Brave New World Revisited*, by Huxley—and a Hair-Do magazine. David is reading *Donner Pass*, by Stewart, *Storm*, by Stewart, *Fire*, by Stewart, and a few others by Stewart. Also a magazine ($1.50!) *The Scientific American*. From the latter he learns how we descended from common ancestors with the ape. Our bookshelf is overflowing— we need another redwood board.

• • • •

No baby yet. We're so poor I'm out of the baby mood. We made a burlap-covered telephone bench, and before we got to use it they shut our phone off.

The baby thing is so hopeless. The hormone pills didn't do a damn thing. Our odds are 1 out of 125, or once every 15 months the odds are with us. Then there's another complication—my temperature chart isn't registering like the sample one. Either I am dead, or the thermometer is broken. Any wonder I don't feel like pounding on doors in Hollywood! This is more important to me than acting. I'm so desperate I've even started praying, and I don't believe in it! But just in case there is a God up there who listens to us tiny humans' troubles, I'm trying. You know, leaving no stone unturned, that sort of thing.

David's birthday is tomorrow and we don't have any money to get him a present. Guess I'll have to charge something. What a rut we're in.

I've been painting upstairs. I painted the waste-paper basket blue and the top of the chest. David finally finished it. One of the cats knocked over the paint can. What fun we had cleaning it up.

I'm doing *Lower Depths* by Gorkey. All the women's parts are good—so wish me luck!

*   *   *   *

Just a note—things have been happening around here, for the better. Hurrah! David took his paintings to four galleries and three of the four like them! We've sold one painting for $100. Also he gets a one man show in the fall. He's doing cartoons now, too— has sent them to *Look, Post, New Yorker,* and *Playboy. Post* rejected them and we haven't heard from the others yet. The cartoons are funny, too.

More good news! David's sperm count jumped from 21,000,000 to 51,000,000. We don't know why, we're just thankful.

I have an agent! Might be going to Las Vegas for six weeks as a dancer ($145 a week)! It would be at the Dunes. Nothing is definite. . . .

*   *   *   *

We've moved at last. We got a cute upper with a small kitchen. The bathroom is much like the last one, except this toilet works. We've come up in the world. There is a hole in the hall which leads to a big attic that will be David's work room. Of course we'll have to get a rope ladder!

Bad news. Our little Putt-Putt was run over about three weeks ago. We ran an ad for him in the paper, and finally I called the refuse department and they remembered picking up a white cat.

We've been moving for two weeks so I haven't tried modeling yet. I'm going to have pictures taken tomorrow night. Going to H'wood Friday to see three photographers.

My mother called this morning—she only calls when someone dies. This time it was my little great-grandmother. She was in her eighties and stone-blind.

Oh, yes, I was inseminated (Wow) this month and then got my period with all its glorious cramps and pain. So we try again next month. It didn't hurt a bit but I sure felt like a cow or something. Very unromantic. David keeps telling me patience is a virtue— HA!

We have a *red* phone. Getting awfully materialistic lately.

· · · ·

AT LAST! HURRAH! IT HAPPENED. A BABY! HOT DAMN! GOING TO BE A MOTHER! We did it! I am now one month pregnant. HA! HA! HA! HA! I have all the signs. Monday I was threatening to miscarry—there's a chance we'll lose it—cross your fingers for us. I'd die if anything happened now. We're floating, dancing, singing—*the impossible happened!* —in only two tries. I have gas pains, sore breasts, and love every minute of it!

Do you realize our baby is ½ of an inch long this week—visible to the naked eye. (Girl, of course.) But that's not all. This week her backbone is being formed. But wow! Next week, real progress. The depressions are being formed where her eyes will be. All that inside me. Imagine.

I lost four pounds. I still may be able to go to Las Vegas. I passed the dance auditions with flying colors. We'll see what the doctor says.

Three magazines rejected David's cartoons. They were funny, too. He took his canvases to several galleries and got a terrific response. He converted the attic and I never see him anymore.

I hope someday you will be this gloriously, ridiculously happy as we are now. I just go around laughing all the time. I keep thinking, Ha! Ha! I've got a secret.

* * * *

Gas pains, cramps, nausea all gone, but I have quite an odd assortment of aches and pains which crop up regularly. My back aches occasionly, I'm not allowed to smoke when my back aches and was told to cut down. So I did.

We're invited to a nudist camp this weekend. What a riot!

You'd be proud of me—I'm making all of my maternity clothes. Baby is five inches long! Progress!

* * * *

Well, I'm four-and-a-half months pregnant and the baby has been kicking for three weeks. What a thrill. I can't tell you how it makes me feel.

Baby is ten inches long now! My breasts drip occasionally. (Are bigger, too! Hurrah!) "Wee Thing" kicks and it jars my whole stomach. I love every minute of it. It all makes me feel so important.

. . . .

A change in plans! All this weight I've gained is evidently salt water and so the doctor wants to induce the baby earlier—Saturday the twenty-first is the big day! If she is a girl, we'll name her "Kie."

. . . .

You won't know Kie—she's got a wee bit more hair now and she slides all around on her tummy. Today she was sitting in her stroller and pulled herself up and stood there. I nearly burst my buttons! She'll be walking soon. . . .

Others babies are adorable, but this one is "special." Sounds like what every mother would say, right? Now, how to put this in words?—I know that she is somehow *different*. When I look at her, she responds like any other baby, but in her eyes I can see, sense, feel a *knowing*. She *knows* something. I don't know what it is, but she has answers, or a knowledge that I don't have. Other people don't believe or understand me. Do you?

· · · ·

Kie fell off the washing machine yesterday—she cried and I cried, but we will both survive. . . .

David and I hardly ever fight anymore. When we do it's only a half-hearted attempt, just to have something to do besides neck.

· · · ·

Kie can ride her trike now.
We're going to Ohio for Easter . . . wish us luck!

· · · ·

I can't write straight as I'm kept on shots and tranquilizers all the time. I can bear it this way, but when they wear off I go to pieces. I must get over this soon. I know I can't live on pills.

We're so thankful that Kie was *killed* instantly. I can hardly bear to write that word. I never even saw her again after the accident. So many thoughts run through my mind. If only I could stop thinking. Oh, what can we do? The pain won't go away. I put it out of my mind for awhile but whenever I'm alone it comes, and I miss her so awful much. I think if I could just love her and kiss her one more time. Really, we loved her almost as if we knew she would be taken away. I wonder if this is what she knew? Is this what I saw in her eyes?

We're grateful to have had her even that long.

But, oh, it wasn't enough! We wanted her so badly forever.

They say the funeral was "lovely." So many flowers and people. I try not to think about it. All I can think over and over again is Kie is gone for ever and ever and ever and I can't bear it. . . .

.   .   .   .

It's been three weeks today. David and I have come to one conclusion. We believe—by faith alone—that somewhere, in some form, she is still alive. Oh, I wish we could tell you the feelings we have. I feel I'm beginning to accept her death and I *don't want to!* I feel guilty for letting that precious darling slip away from me so easily. It seems like we have been robbed of the chance to fight for her life. It was so quick. In her death we weren't even given a chance to fight with all our guts for her. And I'm beginning to feel bitter about that.

Another thing. It tears me in two to see a small blond girl playing. I can feel the bitterness creeping in. Why Kie and not her? Why not the grotesque old lady across the street, who lives on and on and on? Why Kie and not me? Why? Why? Why?

I hope this feeling passes soon, because it is a hate feeling and wrong. Nothing about Kie had any hate in it.

The very worst is just plain missing her. I keep thinking she's at a baby-sitter's, and I'm anxious to pick her up and bring her home. Oh my God, how I miss her.

We finally went to her grave (I hate that word) yesterday. It was the hardest thing I have ever done.

It wasn't marked yet, and there were several new graves. We had trouble finding it—we were almost frantic, then we decided on one because it was so small.

I shouldn't dwell on these things or I'll lose what mind I have left.

•　　•　　•　　•

Almost six weeks and the hurt is still so fresh. Help, help—I just can't let her go. Whatever will I do? Sunday I'm going up to the cemetery to be with her again. It's like a magnet drawing me there. I don't approve of these things, but somehow it's different when it's your own baby there.

Oh dear, I was feeling better today, and now I started thinking again. If only the mind could be shut off.

Wasn't she a little special? I mean by *special*, a quality about her—perhaps love. She was so full of love. She seemed to radiate it.

Oh dear—again!

•　　•　　•　　•

The nightmares are terrible. Last night we were at my grandma's in Greenville. I was sleeping alone in a strange room, and I got so scared! I felt Kie was right out there in the dark and could come in if I opened the window. Half of me seemed to wait for her and half of me was terrified she might come. I didn't sleep a wink until three A.M. when I got Mother to come in with me. The nights are worst. I'm so filled up with a hurt that won't go away! Sometimes I just want to scream and rant and rave, and I have to go on behaving normally—as if everything were all right.

It's time for bed again and I dread it.

•　•　•　•

Jenny's afterthoughts:

I felt a great need afterward to talk about her, so I did, compulsively, to everyone who would listen. I think that helped me eventually to *let go*. Everybody was wonderful and they did all they could, but I craved something more. It was *touching*, it was the empathy of someone who *really* understood my feelings I needed. I found it with David and with a neighbor who had lost her son. It was like we were a club.

We needed to talk to others who had experienced this. When we talked, we said volumes with a phrase, or a look, a pat, or a hug. We needed to cry with someone.

David and I clung to each other like animals for months. We grieved together. When he woke up crying in the night, I comforted him, and he did the same for me. The bond we created sharing our loss of Kie was (and is) stronger than *any other* we share. Nothing, not love, sex, friendship or marriage vows, is as meaningful as our experience together over Kie.

•　•　•　•

Did you know real people wring their hands? I did, for months. I walked the floors and cried and sort of "washed my hands."

Suicide seemed so nice at times.

Letting go is the only way to survive. There were still reasons to live, so I chose to live. There was no other choice. I let her go.

Then, of course, there was the guilt to deal with. The most precious person in my life (then or now) was gone, without a word from me. I felt I had let her down. How dare I be happy again? Or love, or feel, or plan again? And most damning: how dare I *forget*? "Oh, that's wrong," I kept telling myself. "If I could let her go that must mean I never *really* loved her." Now I see how distorted that was.

Kie is now where she "ought" to be. Part of my dearest memory. I don't dare think of her too often. See what you asked of me? Shame on you.

I can't deny I grew (changed — perhaps) but hopefully I would have anyway. Some of us take a long, long time to grow. It's Hell. Maybe that's all there is.

• • • •

Ulla-lulla

She is gone, forever
and ever the dim day breaks
and ever the day miscarries.
Bang your head upon the wall,
kick and shout and rage,

scream, weep tears and pray,
fly out in fury, revolt,
    surrender, withdraw, lie down
    like a stone.

It will not go away.
    Nothing changes.
    Nothing changes,
though the stripped rim of the heart break
    and the see-saw prattle and clack
    of the barefoot dead
    scold, cast blame, accuse;

    Oh my God it's time for bed again,
    my God, it's time for bed!

twelve

DOCTOR SONTAG, EXCISING a second spot for biopsy under local anesthesia, makes a small incision in my arm and accidentally severs an artery. Blood spurts, and spurts, and spurts with each heartbeat, covering his gloves, his chest, his table, his nurse, and his wall.

"Oooops," he says, never dropping a stitch, never losing his poise.

I am embarrassed at having made such a mess, although I know very well it was not my fault. The nurse, in a stiffening red gown, applies a pressure bandage to my incision to stop the profuse bleeding.

In prehistoric days, the skulls of ancient men were trepanned, presumably without anesthetic, to combat headaches, epilepsy, and to obtain polished roundels for use as good-luck amulets. Some skulls show as many as seven holes. Apparently many of them survived the surgery.

It was not always easy for the surgeons, either. According to the Code of Hammurabi, laws inscribed on stone dictated that if a surgeon caused the death of a man, his fingers would be cut off. Such a law must have made physicians more careful—or maybe the prints of multilated hands and evidence of chopped-off fingers in Mark's *Study of Human Skeletal Remains* were not a magical appeasement for ancient gods or devils, as the book supposes, but evidence of clumsy surgeons.

Medieval and Renaissance surgeries, like prehistoric operations, were bloodbaths. People died screaming in hideous agony, while surgeons literally tore their bodies apart.

They still die screaming. Such pain obliterates all embarrassment. It is this indignity that frightens me most. Death, I might be able to handle. But unrelenting, terrible pain and gradual deterioration—never. Perhaps Longfellow was right saying, "Whom the gods wish to destroy, they first make mad" Randall Jarrell wrote in *90 North*:

> The world—my world spins on this final point
> Of cold and wretchedness: all lines, all winds
> End in this whirlpool I at last discover.
> And it is meaningless. . . .
>
> I see at last that all the knowledge
> I wrung from the darkness—that the darkness flung me—
> Is worthless as ignorance: nothing comes from nothing
> The darkness from the darkness. Pain comes from the darkness,
> And we call it wisdom. It is pain.

It is Hell. Maybe that is all there is. I hope not.

The pathology report says this specimen is benign. Thank you, God.

thirteen

IN JUST—
      spring   it's raining and gray. With all my love to e. e. cummings, the world is "mud-luscious" and "puddle- wonderful." The air smells of dripping pine trees, woodsmoke and liquid earth. I do love the smell of mud. I'd like to run barefoot through the mudpuddles, and roll in them like a hippopotamus, and breathe them, and even eat them! Wouldn't the boys love that? Today would be remembered for all time as The Day Mom Went Berserk And Ate The Whole Front Yard.

The boys dance like water sprites, open-mouthed, fingers spread wide to catch the drops. They sail stick boats down the raingutters at floodtide, hair sopped and eyelashes dripping water. They stalk precious stones. and iron nails, and beetles in the muddy yard. They are their father's sons. Maybe this is The Day They Will Find A Fossil!—a shark's tooth, a trilobite, or maybe an Indian arrowhead. They hide in the shadows and in wet dark places around the black trunks of trees, in the sharp angles of walls, under the neighbor's pruned hedges, the wild light on them silvering reluctantly as the sun tries to shine.

Wonder of all wonders, a rainbow! Remy lifts a finger to test the direction of the wind, as Balboa on the mountain above the Pacific must have tested the world-shaking wind upon his finger.

Ah, well. Remy hides his stiff fingers inside the warmer sleeves of his coat. The wind is cold. They play until time and chattering teeth drive them inside.

Sunday. Where are the churchbells? Our church has no bell tower. Churches now are large places of polished pews, thick glass doors and bricks. No bells. They used to be homey, dusty places of peeling wood and white-steepled bells that rang out Sundays, or marriages, or funerals. They kept their dead beside them close in little churchyard cemeteries. I suppose their numbers grew too large. The multitudinous dead kept coming on, like the sad march of the Cheyenne to reservations. The dead have all been exiled to reservations of their own called Graceland, and Elysian Gardens, and Mount Olivet.

Is there truly a God? I hope there is—some loving, all-powerful parent who blows the spark of my life tenderly, who knows me intimately and values me as the apple of His eye.

The rainbow doubles and vanishes.

We walk to church in the afterglow. The boys run fast and far ahead of me. There, the choir sings:

God moves in a mysterious way, His wonders to perform;
He plants his footsteps in the sea,
And rides upon the storm.

Deep in unfathomable mines Of never failing skill,
He treasures up his bright designs
And works his sovereign will.

His purposes will ripen fast, Unfolding every hour.
The bud may have a bitter taste,
But sweet will be the flower.

An ordinary man in Pirandello's *The Man With The Flower In His Mouth*, says,

Death passed my way. It planted this flower in my mouth and said to me, 'Keep it, friend. I'll be back. . . .'

There is a flower from death in all our mouths.

·   ·   ·   ·

Another solitary pleasure of mine is looking at photographs in the albums. Many of the pictures are older than I am.

There are stout, blue-eyed great-grandmothers and stern, bearded great-grandfathers. This one fought in the civil war. He was a prisoner-of-war at Andersonville, in North Carolina. He had a bullet in the calf of his leg for the rest of his life.

This one had two wives at once, one twenty years younger than the other. I wonder what great-grandma thought of the new young wife?

My grandma, aged sixteen. She was red-haired and beautiful.

There is Daddy as a boy in Utah, riding bareback on a horse he called "Old Chub."

And Daddy as a young man. He could have been a movie star. He looks like a young Gary Cooper.

Mama, back when she was called "Pinky" for her red hair. I wish I had known her then.

And me, as an infant in a lace bonnet.

Me, again, wearing a paper clown suit. What a show-off!

My graduation picture.

Here's Mark in the Navy, in Japan. Wow. I wish I had known him then! He had the face of an angel.

Jenny, her arms loaded with costumes from *Italian Straw Hat*.

Jenny dancing with a white cat.

Mark again, at the beach, roasting a hot dog over a fire at Corona Del Mar. How young he is. Look how much hair he has!

Some pictures from the road—nylons and a bra drying on some hotel radiator.

Some wedding pictures. Mark cutting our wedding cake with a pancake turner. Why didn't we have a knife? I have forgotten.

Jenny and me, smiling. "You be good to her now," she warned Mark. No one ever said to me, "You be good to him." At least I don't remember it if they did.

Ensenada's famous blowhole, *La Bufadora*. We went to Mexico on our honeymoon, ran out of money and lived for an entire week on corn tortillas, goat's butter, and 7-Up! I never had so much fun in my whole life. We were poor but happy. The village idiots.

Me on the bed, holding Remy, aged 3 weeks. I had super legs then.

Remy's first bath.

Remy (crying) and Mickey Mouse at Disneyland.

Me again, wheeled out of the delivery room holding a new baby still covered with white vernix.

Pictures of Christmases and Easters, snowmen and sand-castles, birthday parties, feeding peanuts to the elephants at the zoo. The albums are full. There are boxes of loose pictures. I always intended to buy another album and start over. Another good intention. I return the albums to the bookcase, take a long hot bubblebath full of Emeraude, and go to bed.

I dream of binary stars, circling one another like two dogs ready to fight. One of the stars explodes and becomes a supernova, and then a black hole, and all the bright substance of the other star is sucked and whirled into the hole like water whirling down a drain.

I always dream in color, with a wide screen and stereophonic sound. Some people say they do not dream at all. What a pity. What a waste of time, to sleep and not dream. I dream asleep or awake.

Not all dreams are pleasant. Years ago, while traveling around the country with the road company, I used to dream that I was a performer in a play, but I was unable to remember what the play was, or what role I was expected to play, or any of the lines. I ran around backstage, looking frantically for a script, and when I finally found one, I had forgotten how to read!

I sometimes write great poetry while I sleep. I can't usually recall any of it. But once, I wrote it down before it dissolved in daylight:

We had but one thing for dinner,
a tooth,
and that was passed around
several times
before it was clipped down.

Many great and important people
sat
at either end of the table
discussing
whether it is nobler to live
or to die.

What was the question?
I forget.
What is the answer?

Look out, T. S. Here I come!

fourteen

WE HAVE A CAT. REMY found a skinny kitten shivering and soaked from the storm. He fixed her a bowl of warm milk, but she wouldn't drink. She is yellow and white—not more than eight or ten weeks old.

I think the kitten is sick. I wrap her warmly in a small towel, but she continues to shiver. I try to feed her with an eyedropper. Not much luck. She is limp, and I can feel her heart racing under her skinny ribs. She opens her mouth to 'meow' but rattles instead.

She is dying. Her heart still beats, rapid and feeble, and she lies quietly as I stroke her head.

Three days later the kitten is dead. Remy and Chris weep. We bury her in the back yard, wrapped in the little towel, onto which I have pinned a note:

All things bright and beautiful,
All creatures great and small,
All things wise and wonderful,
The Lord God made them all.

The boys are not comforted. I put my arms around them and we all three weep.

Vonnegut's Tralfamadorians, seeing into the fourth dimension, perceive the universe in a radically different way.

> All moments, past, present, and future, always have existed, always will exist. The Tralfamadorians can look at all the different moments just the way we can look at a stretch of the Rocky Mountains, for instance. They can see how permanent all the moments are, and they can look at any moment that interests them. It is just an illusion we have here on Earth that one moment follows another, like beads on a string, and that once a moment is gone it is gone forever.
>
> When a Tralfamadorian sees a corpse, all he thinks is that the dead person is in bad condition at that particular moment, but that the same person is just fine in plenty of other moments. Now, when I myself hear that somebody is dead, I simply shrug and say what the Tralfamadorians say about dead people, which is "So it goes!"

So it goes. I am three years old and they have taken me to say "goodbye" to my grandpa, who is sleeping in flowers, but he doesn't wake no matter what is said to him.

Then I am six years old, having another encounter with vulture Death. I hold a brown leather dog collar. Sparky was a good dog, now he is dead, run over by an ice-cream truck. The ice-cream truck meant no harm. The driver was sorry, and he said so.

"I am sorry the kitty died," I say, tucking the boys into bed.

"I am sorry, too," Remy whispers. "I prayed she would get better. I thought she might."

"It hurts her to be dead?" asks Chris.

"No, it doesn't hurt her," I say. (What the hell do I know about being dead?) "The poor kitty is better off," I tell him.

"Oh," he says, gazing at me with his trusting light-colored eyes.

"I wish she was still alive," says Remy.

"I wish she was, too." I hug them all goodnight. In some matters of great importance there are no right words.

Ten P.M. There is a full moon. Somewhere far down the block a dog barks.

A television newscaster reports in a monotone: "A nine-year veteran police officer, near death Friday from self-inflicted gunshot wounds to the head, is considered by police as a prime suspect in more than thirty rapes, robberies and assaults since last August. The officer was in critical condition at Mount Carmel Mercy Hospital after putting his revolver to his head and pulling the trigger as two officers approached to question him . . .

"A bomb blew out the lavatory of a Phillippine jetliner flying at 24,000 feet Friday, and the man who had apparently carried the explosive aboard was blown out of the plane, aviation officials reported . . .

"Stocks were higher Friday, in response to favorable economic reports. Trading was moderate. The Dow Jones industrial average down a point at the outset, was ahead 5.72 points . . .

"Fair and chilly Friday night and mostly sunny Saturday."

And so on . . . and so on.

The dog barks again. "So it goes."

I slip my arms around Mark and lay my head against his chest. His thumb makes little circles up and down my back. The baby kicks and twists.

"Do you feel that?" I roll over and put his hand on my belly. He laughs softly, caressing me. The Mountain meets Mohammed.

The bedroom door bangs open. Matthew's plaintive voice comes through the half-light from the hall. "Had a attident," he confesses sleepily. "I co-o-old." He drops his wet pants on the floor and settles himself damply between me and Mark.

"I think Matthew's had an accident," I say. Mark makes loud snoring noises.

"A spider's in my bed," Matthew adds.

I change his pants and bed. I show him, inch by inch, that no spiders share his sheets.

"Where is Popeye's teeth?" he asks.

"Whose teeth?"

"Does Popeye got teeth?"

"Matthew, it's late," I say. "Who knows?"

I crawl back into bed. "Mark?" I whisper. Rats, he really is asleep. Oh, well. I'm out of the mood now anyway. But I can't sleep.

Does Popeye have teeth?

fifteen

APRIL 28—OUR SEVENTH
wedding anniversary! The weather has warmed beautifully,
and Mark has tickets to a concert at the University Fine
Arts Center's Lyceum Series. We don't go out much and I
am excited and glad. It will be the first live concert we've
been to in years. In celebration of the event I had my hair
cut short. There was already so much short stubble in with
the long hair I decided to give it all an even chance. I'm a
firm believer in even chances. Mark likes it short, but I
hardly recognize myself when I pass a mirror. I look like
Little Orphan Annie—sans the coins on the eyes.

Eleven A.M. The mailman brings a doctor bill advising
me to complete the thirteen questions on the standard
insurance form and mail it to my insurance company. Exam,
extended:—A.N.A., Latex Fixation, Hemogram WBC, T4,
T3/T4, CS25/ Hem/T4, TSH, and RIA—$117.55.

There is also an advertisement for a $150,000.00 Cancer
Plan. *Plan on cancer, anyone?* Coverage is guaranteed to you

and your family members who have not had Cancer. With a capital C. "Cancer is so horrible and dreaded a disease," says the brochure, "that the normal reaction is to say 'it can't happen to me.'" It tells the "sad truth" about Babe Ruth, Jack Benny, Walt Disney, Gypsy Rose Lee, Sophie Tucker, Vince Lombardi, Nat "King" Cole, Senator Hubert Humphrey, and others: "For every celebrity struck by Cancer (capital C again), there are countless other Americans who are also being struck—ordinary folks like you and me." Who's *ordinary*? Not me! The late Senator Humphrey warns, "Only a few millionaires can afford cancer." Well, thank God. That certainly lets me out. What a relief! I throw the application in the trash, but it has upset me.

Let me forget about cancer and pain and dying for a little while. Let me not see any more cheap newspapers with headlines that announce "New Breakthrough in Cancer Cures." Let me not read any more magazine pieces on Laetrile. And let me not listen to any more of the dreadful tales I'm forever and forever told of friends of friends who are "terminal" and not expected to live past Tuesday, or who have already died. In the obituaries, however, I notice people still do die of things besides cancer. Old age, auto-pedestrian accidents, heart attacks. An old poet wrote: "Death has a thousand doors for men to take their exit . . ." I only hear of ONE.

Annie from next door tells me how her Uncle Jack's ("You remember my telling you about my Uncle Jack?") cancer has spread to his bones now. She details his suffering, and his doctor's inadequacies, and how he waits in agony for the shots of morphine they will not give, whimpering, begging for pills, for a gun, for a knife, for *anything*.

I try to be philosophical. But what in the name of heaven and all the angels do Annie's Uncle Jack, and Sophie Tucker and Babe Ruth have to do with me? Can't they see I don't need any more ghost stories! Can't they feel how vulnerable I am?—Badly scotch-taped together.

The day is spoiled. Rats.

I am surprised at my anger. Why am I so angry? Maybe I am just tired and overly pregnant.

Freeze. Let everything stay just as it is, forever. *Freeze*. Children, stop growing! Hair and fingernails, stop! Nerves and muscles and cells, stop! Old people: not one more wrinkle, you hear? Not one more white hair! *Freeze*. Clocks and trains and dinners on the stove, stone-cold bubbles in the stew, half-baked pies in stone-cold ovens, doors half-slammed, mouths half-open to speak. Everybody, stop! *Freeze*!

I worry most about my inability to bear pain. I have read about a doctor in London who mixes heroin and cocaine "cocktails" which keep her dying patients alert and pain-free. Such drugs are illegal here. London, here I come.

A portrait of fear: I am eight years old. Fear is running up the street for home with a big dog barking behind me, showing his long teeth. Fear is listening to the sighs and groans the wind makes in the stovepipe. Fear is waiting for trees to grow out of my stomach from apple-seeds I swallowed.

Fear, today, is waiting for dragons to sprout somewhere in my brain, in my lungs or bones, from impious seeds I swallowed yesterday. Does God punish mindless irreverent lapses of youthful behavior so harshly? The question still haunts me. I'm sorry, okay? I'm sorry. I'm *sorry*!

I don't think that has anything to do with it. Or do I?

109

At sundown we walk up the hill to the University. The evening is pleasant, and Mark holds my hand all the way.

The pianist's performance is sensitive and exciting. He plays Tchaikovsky's *Theme and Variations, Op. 19, No. 6,* a Prokofiev sonata that is controlled and articulate, and a romantic Chopin sonata, lyrical and lovely. He does Rachmaninoff as an encore, and another short Chopin. Mark listens intently, completely absorbed in the music. His face is relaxed and happy.

And we walk home. On the way we stop for pizza and cold mugs of root beet. I feel mellow and sentimental.

"It's been really good, hasn't it, these seven years," I say. "I mean, everything. All the time."

"It *is* good," Mark agrees.

"Mark, I'm glad you love me." And finally I find the courage to say what has been unspoken in my mind for months. "What will you do if I die?" There. I have never said that word aloud to him before.

"I've never considered that possibility," he says.

"Maybe you should." I blow the paper from my straw at him. "You would get married again, wouldn't you?"

A terrible pang of bilious jealousy rages through me, that some other woman should have my children, and my kitchen, my bed and my pillow. I try to imagine Mark in bed with her, making love to her. I inhale hurt and rage. Unexpected tears run down my cheeks and quickly I wipe them away. "Mark, listen to me. You're not listening to me."

"Then stop being so silly."

"It's not silly. It's practical. Who would you marry? I have to know. Not Annelise?"

"Not Annelise. Nobody." His face is puzzled and nervous. "Why nobody?"

"Because I love *you*." He blows the paper from his straw at me.

"I love you more," I say. "Do you know what I wish? I wish we had made love that night in the park—out in the open, in the grass under the stars. Why didn't we?"

"Because you were afraid we'd be mugged," he says.

"Mark, if I die, I'm going to miss you like crazy." The pain of separation whirls through me like a dry wind. "I miss you already." Can he feel it? No. I feel betrayed. By my own body. By Mark, who will certainly marry again and will probably be blissfully happy with someone much younger and prettier than I am. By my children, who will love another mother.

And that's how it should be! But, oh, how it hurts.

Mark doesn't want to talk about it. It makes him uncomfortable.

"I'm sorry," I say. "The only thing is, I'm a little bit scared."

"Don't be," he says, squeezing my hand. "We'll take it one day at a time."

All right. One day at a time.

•   •   •   •

Avaler des Couleuveres*

**To Swallow Snakes*

> *From pole to pole the pit is black:*
> *Unconquered, conquered, back to back,*
> *My soul and the night that covers me,*
> *Whoever the gods, wherever they be.*

Fate has bludgeoned and tricked and tried.
My children weep, and I have cried
And bargained and prayed, denied and bled
And lost. I bow my bloody head.

Within this place of wrath and tears
The horror looms above the fears.
Beyond the cowering, trembling dread
Find the startled, timid Dead.

It matters not how straight the gate,
How blessed with sacraments the scroll—
My life is rot and rust and hate!
Azrael is Master of my soul.

*(My apologies to William Ernest Henley who wrote
INVICTUS.)*

•   •   •   •

Out of that black mood, I think. Thank goodness they
don't come too often. I will not "sup full of horrors" again
today. *I will stay healthy.* Last night's Rachmaninoff runs
through my head with clear and clean precision.

I had another strange dream last night. I had a child's
picture book with the title "Christ Walked Among the
Crucified." Inside, there was a picture of a huge tree, no
leaves, but many long thorns—and upon each thorn, impaled
at the middle was a man, woman, or child, doubled over in
agony. The next page showed the same people, smiling, and
all with little bandages in their middles where the thorns
had been removed. The text said: "And with His touch, He

healed the wounds of those who died *for Him.*"

What does that mean, I wonder? Most likely nothing. I ought to get a book on the interpretation of dreams. What would Doctor Freud say?

Be not afraid?

sixteen

I AM NOT ANGRY ANY more. But I think that being angry is better than being afraid.

I have bad lower back pains (which I, of course, attribute to advancing pregnancy, what else?) At seven months, the baby could conceivably live if something happened to me and he were taken. But he probably wouldn't. He needs *the whole nine months*! Then—if I must—I will die. Okay? Okay.

This last thought shocks me.

But I am not at all apprehensive about my doctor's appointment tomorrow. Not much.

•   •   •   •

En route to the examining table I meet a handsome young man who has Hodgkin's Disease. His name is Eddie. He says this is his last visit.

"Good for you!" I tell him. But it's not so good. His treatments, besides having made him sterile, are unbearable.

"I've quit relying so much on orthodox medicine. Radiation and chemotherapy are Hell," he says. "Literal Hell."

"What will you do instead?" I ask him.

"I've been eating better, watching my diet. Chaparrel tea and apricot pits have helped the most."

Chaparrel tea and apricot pits! Eddie tells me he is twenty-two years old. And he has consigned himself into the care of tea and apricot pits! I know that Hodgkin's Disease is one of the more controllable forms of cancer. Radiation and nitrogen mustard are surely not pleasant, but tea and apricot pits! How many of "us" would jump at having his chance of living for another twenty years with any amount of temporary discomfort, (even Hell!) from "orthodox" treatment. And he's giving up. *Bon voyage*, Eddie. I wish you well.

I take time out to look around me. I see a few people I've seen here before. We are like members of an exclusive club. With very high dues. Except for Eddie, most of them are old. I wonder if I will ever be so old?

Everything's fine. I did not mention the back pain to Doctor Sontag. It seemed better to let sleeping dogs lie.

Boy, now *that's* stupid! *Bon voyage*, Mrs. Harper.

seventeen

MY MOTHER HAS DIS-
covered a lump coming almost opposite a tiny indentation
on her breast. She showed it to her doctor. He looked
carefully, but he couldn't see what she saw. He thought she
was imagining it, but finally he noticed the nipple tipping
slightly, so they decided to be on the safe side and do a
biopsy. They told her not to worry—nine times out of ten
these things turn out to be benign.

She would not have told me. She would have kept it
from me as I did from her. It was Papa who told me. She is
terrified, but everyone thinks it will be a simple removal of
a benign lump. "I will be in the class with Rosalyn Carter
and be home in an hour," Mama assures me.

It is not benign. It is cancer.

Mama tells me, "I want to cry. To go away someplace,
anyplace—and never come back again."

I feel a dreadful, tight aching in the middle of my chest.
My mother. Mama. Laughing Pinky, the Girl with the Green

Eyes. No one is spared. I think I can detect a hideous faint odor of disinfectant. I open a window for a breath of fresh air. I think I am going to be sick.

•　　•　　•　　•

Annelise brings me down a section from a midnight tabloid. Blessings light upon you, Annie. If I had half a crown a day, I'd gladly spend it on you. The tabloid announces "New Hope For Cancer Victims". A post-operative treatment using a drug and a vaccine in combination has dramatically increased the survival rate for victims of melanoma. The treatment, using chemotherapy and immunotherapy "offers a statistically significant benefit on both disease-free survival and also actual survival," declared Doctor Robert Carey, associate clinical professor of medicine at the Harvard Medical School.

On the next page, between the bust developer—"My bust went from hopeless to fantastic in less than 15 days!"—and "How to Have Your Lucky Number Horoscope Individually Prepared," is an article telling how Jacques Brel has died after a "ten-year battle" with—guess what?

I open this morning's paper. Page one says: "Solvent Stops Cancer Cells—Tested in Mice." Six of them, to be exact. Six tiny, bald, defenseless creatures. Further testing will be done on 50 to 100 more cancer-afflicted mice and if the results are "encouraging" there will be experiments with rabbits, dogs, and monkeys, followed by human trials within three to five years.

Can I wait that long? I have visions of dying, and the following morning's headlines will announce: "CANCER LICKED! Sure Cure Discovered at Last!"

Television's *Good Morning America* yesterday also had an interview with a doctor, a researcher, who explained "custom-blended drugs." The surgeon removes a piece of the patient's cancer, minces it, and injects it into "nude" mice, who then grow that particular individual's cancer. Or else the cancer is cultivated in a laboratory dish and then analyzed, enabling the doctors to treat a specific, individual cancer with various combinations of drugs and choose which has the greatest effect. The doctor bases his research on a theory that the wayward cells can be cured, and need not be killed—a sort of humane penal system of microscopic criminal rehabilitation, I guess. No capital punishment.

•   •   •   •

Mama writes, "I am in the hospital again. I am not in pain, but I am uncomfortable; I can't lie on either side—only on my back. Now I am as flat on one side as on the other."

She has had a second mastectomy. "Last time," she says, "they called it a radical. This time they call it a modified radical, but they both look about the same to me."

I encourage her to talk about her feelings, to write them down. We are able to talk to one another not as parent to child, but now, for the first time, as woman to woman.

"Everything is the same as before," she says. "They have taken out the IV and the little drain that I have carried around with me. I am glad that is over."

"Do your exercises," I tell her over the telephone. "Smile."

Mama says, "When your brother was born, Grandma used to say to me, 'What pretty breasts you have.' And they were. Not too small or too large, and the nipples were small and pink—so small, in fact, that when the breasts were full of milk and hard, the baby could hardly nurse. Later, the nipples began to be inverted, especially on my left side. I had heard about inverted nipples being a sign of cancer, so one time I asked the doctor about them. He wasn't worried. He said to me, 'My mother had inverted nipples all her life and never had cancer.' So I didn't worry about them anymore —much.

"The doctor has been in and talked to me," she says. "He is happy and so am I. All seven of my tests have come back negative, and I am going home."

"It is so good to be home again," she says. "Your Papa cooks our meals. Everything should be fine, but I can't believe that this awful thing has happened to me. I am uncomfortable in this tight paper tape. My arms are numb. I can't sleep—naturally, neither can your Papa. He is very kind and patient, and he tries to comfort me. We get up and drink hot milk and talk. Then after a long time, we go back to bed and maybe sleep a little.

"One day I woke up and I had a pimple on my forehead. I was so frightened," she confesses. "I don't know anything about cancers. Do they get into your bloodstream and spread, and pop out like a pimple sometimes?

"I have a flat chest. That doesn't bother me so much. I am very uninformed about these matters, but I made a sort of camisole out of a slip and I stuff it with nylon scarves. They can be wadded up and they make a nice, light, springy pad that doesn't flatten out or press too heavily. This works fine except that it slides up."

Finally Mama says, "The doctor has given me a prescription for a prosthesis. I bought the kind the saleslady recommended, and a new bra with pockets in it. After

120

wearing nylon scarves, this feels so good and looks good. Now I have a brand new figure! People say, 'How are you?' and I always say, 'I'm just fine.' And I am fine, too, except when I am depressed or can find something to worry about.

"The stitches will gradually go away and the scars will get lighter. My arms will get over being numb and my skin will fit again. I have decided that I am going to quit worrying, to live until I die, be it from pneumonia or from falling down and breaking my neck. I am not ever going to worry again—really!

"But, I wonder now, if that little mole on my leg isn't getting a bit sensitive—and doesn't it look a *little* different?"

•   •   •   •

I have just discovered L. E. Sissman, through reading Violet Weingarten's *Intimations of Mortality* (a "testament of courage and dignity, of life prevailing over death." A fine book—alas! published *after her death*.) Sissman, dying of Eddie's illness, Hodgkin's Disease, was a poet, and had been a reviewer for *The New Yorker*, and wrote a monthly column for *The Atlantic*. The book, *Hello, Darkness*, contains 134 of his poems, which the jacket says were "inspired" by his illness. "There is a powerful rage to live . . ." says the jacket, "even in the face of death." There is also a lot of "suffering of an unpicturesque kind—the kind that takes place in hospitals—which Sissman had a remarkable gift for picturing."

Ah, yes. I remember well "the pinpoint of the least syringe," and "the buttered catheter," and "the IV's lisp and drip," and the "malignant plum" that "turns out to end in -oma." And, yes, he too saw forever after through an "invisible new veil of finity." Forever after being something akin to ten years or so. Given the extra decade, he "wrote like one possessed of a knowledge remote from most of us, the knowledge of real time."

This does seem morbid for such a beautiful May day as this. No, not morbid—sobering.

The day is really lovely, full of robins and sparrows, and a golden water-colored sun. The boys and I go Indian-file through a hole in the fence to the store, buy hot dogs and potato chips for a picnic in the park.

The boys swing and slide, run and die from invisible and unbloody cap-gun wounds, and rise and run again. Today is an UP. I feel good. I lie on the blanket with the sun shining on my back, and munch Bar-B-Q chips and read Sissman:

> I find you guilty of possession of
> The mortal spirit of unstinted love
> For all things animate and otherwise,
> And of the fatal talent to devise
> Live poems expressing it, transcending all
> Obituaries which record your fall.

eighteen

ANOTHER PICNIC, YEARS ago. I am nine years old. My grandmother is still alive. She is here, with her long red hair wrapped around her head in circles of braids. My grandfather has a bottle of Four Roses whisky to keep him company. He celebrates every holiday with a bottle of Four Roses. He sits apart from the rest of us and hums comfortably to himself. In ten years they will both be gone. But today it is all right, today is fine! Tomorrow we will go our several ways, but today we are all together again. Papa cooks hamburgers over an open fire. Blue smoke rises high into the air. Mama helps Grandma with the lemonade and potato salad. My big brother Gary, who is 15 this year, climbs out of the river, says he won't go back in, the water's too cold. He lies on a wide, warm rock to dry out like a lizard in the sun.

Wild blackberries grow all along the river's edge. The water sparkles. I throw little rocks into the water and the circles of ripples widen and run together. I step off the bank and wade out until the cold water is up to my knees. Little silver shivers dance like ripples up my backbone.

Mother calls me to come back. I turn toward the shore and step off into a deep hole. The cold water closes over my head. Water is in my eyes, in my nose, in my mouth and ears. The waterweeds cover me, tangling my legs, pulling me down. I can't see or breathe or think. I can't call out. I can only sputter and cough and flail my arms helplessly.

My big brother comes in after me. I gasp and cling to his neck. When we are safely back on shore, he says, "If you'd been in the air instead of in the water, you'd a been *flying!*"

A list of things I'd like to do before I die.
  1. *Fly. Something at least possible—maybe hang-glide.*
  2. *Ski.*
  3. *Travel in a hot-air balloon.*
Another list, of things I'll miss most.
  1. *Mark.*
  2. *The boys.*
  3. *My family.*
  4. *My pillow.*
  5. *Fresh apples.*
  6. *Cold water.*
  7. *Sunflowers.*
  8. *Birds.*
  9. *Hot baths and perfume and bubbles.*
  10. *Stars.*
  11. *Dreaming (and waking up again, so that I can tell Mark, "I had the strangest dream. I dreamed I was dead . . ." and he will laugh about it. And we'll sit down and have hot chocolate and cinnamon toast together.)*

nineteen

A LETTER COMES FROM
Jenny saying she is going to the east coast for an audition—
and she'll stop by on the way, *if it is all right*! She writes:

Just a few things I think you should be aware of
before we get together. (Damn, that sounds good!) I
will need:

1. A comfortable bed (satin sheets, if you have them)
   —I plan to sleep 'til at least noon.
2. Breakfast in bed. Orange juice, two eggs, sausage,
   toast—oh, you know.
3. *Please* keep the children quiet at all times! (I certainly hope the baby doesn't cry!)
4. I dress for dinner at 8:00 (with several cocktails
   before. I do hope you won't interfere with my
   religious freedom).
5. Expect you to be dressed in the latest high-fashion
   clothes. I am!

HA! Now for the real list:
1. Don't worry.
2. Don't clean.
3. I'll eat anything—even yogurt, if you like. And I want to take you out to dinner.
4. If you are fat, I'll still love you. (Poverty and kids do that!) I'm fat too. I managed to gain eight pounds. However, yesterday I started on a strict starvation diet. I will lose twelve pounds before I see you. I'll probably be so weak I won't be able to hold my head up—but lovely!

I survey myself in the mirror. "I wish I had never cut my hair. Just look at it." And twenty pounds overweight. I certainly haven't been fading away. Oh, grief! I try to hold my stomach in. It is impossible.

"Your hair looks fine," Mark says.

"I have bags under my eyes." I try to fluff up my hair with the hand dryer. "And I'm so fat."

"Jenny knows you didn't always have the great body you have now." Mark winks at me and smiles. "Besides, you're pregnant. you're supposed to be fat."

"Not *this* fat! My legs aren't pregnant. My chins aren't pregnant." I remember the months and months Jenny and I lived—slimly—on amphetamines, and little else.

"Maybe Jenny is fat," Mark offers, zipping the back of my dress.

"Never." Seven years. people change a lot in seven years. Marriage, babies, other ambitions. But Jenny's ambitions never changed. She is still an actress first. Theatre was still her life, even after she married David. When her baby died it was two years before she could act again. She had a sporadic love affair with a producer, and a breakdown which ended in the psychiatric wing of a hospital. She sat for weeks in the dark, mourning, refusing to allow the shades to

126

be raised, before she went back to David, and to the theatre. Now she is probably better than ever. I wonder if she is as nervous about this reunion as I am?

"Jenny!"

"Jody! Is it you?" A smile breaks accross her face, dimpling her cheeks, and the years drop away. Her hair is no longer red, but jet-black. Except for that she is the same. "It's been a long, long time!"

We rush into each others' arms with an almost painful joy, hugging, laughing, talking too loud and too fast to understand. Then she says, "Gee, you look just the same—from the neck up!"

Embarrassed, I laugh and hug her again. "You're still beautiful."

"How are you?" She looks at me carefully.

"I'm fine . . . fat . . . happy. . . ." I tell her.

"Really?""

"Really."

"You look well."

"I am super!" Only a slight exaggeration. My back is killing me. (I hope that is no more than a figure of speech.) "I'm okay," I say. "I have a very healthy will to live. I just don't make any long-term plans."

"I'm glad you're okay," she says. A pause.

There isn't anything else to say, is there? After seven long years there ought to be many things, marvelous things, loving, earth-shaking, significant things to say. I can't think of any of them.

She sighs. "You had the most beautiful soul of anybody I ever knew."

"Had? Past tense?"

"Have. Present tense." She hugs me again. "Oh, it's so good to see you!"

She takes me to dinner, and then to the ballet. The dancers move easily. Their young bodies are lean and athletic and starkly beautiful under the golden stage lights. They are as enchanted and graceful and responsive as if nothing will ever go wrong—as if they will never get old or soft or scarred.

"Aren't they gorgeous?" I whisper to her. "They are so *beautiful.*"

"Can you believe we ever looked like that?" She leans toward me in the darkness. "We could've been as good as that!"

"You might have. Not me. I never looked that good. If I did, it was a million years ago."

She bursts into laughter.

"Shhhhh!" Says a gentleman in back of us.

After the last curtain call, after the smiles, the adoration and the cheering, the audience moves out of the rows and up the aisles into the outside lobby.

"How long can you stay?" I ask her. "I don't want to waste a minute!"

"I have an audition in New York a week from Monday. It's mainly acting. Not much dancing. Damn, I hope I get it. Lately I've been doing nothing but commercials and voice work," she says. "Jody, would you like to be acting?"

"No. I'm happy writing. I've been lucky. And I have this fantastic editor who thinks I'm a real writer."

"You are," Jenny says. "You were always the strong one. I wanted so much to be *somebody*. It never mattered so much with you. You didn't really care."

Jenny is right. I loved the amber magic of the lights, the make-up and the costumes . . . and the *applause.* If I live to be a hundred I will never fill that void. But I was never possessed by it, as she is. I didn't care *enough*.

She wants to stop for drinks. "I thought you were drinking less," I say.

"Oh, I am! But this is special."

"Do you remember the night you locked yourself in the bathroom?" She stirs her daiquiri with her finger.

"I was a real klutz, wasn't I? For six hours I wrote poems all over the toilet paper, until you finally came home and rescued me."

"Jody, I've saved it. All these years."

"Saved what?"

"The toilet paper with the poetry on it. Someday you'll be famous and I'll have an original." She giggles through the mist. "Hey," she says, her eyes widening suddenly. "Did you see Paul the other night on TV? A small part on Mannix—a rerun."

"No, I didn't."

"Beautiful Paul. He was really very good."

"Really."

I dawdle over my 7-Up, playing with the ice. "Paul was—an opportunist. I don't think about that anymore."

"Do you ever hear from him?"

"Why would I hear from him? No."

"Paul was a son-of-a-bitch," she says bluntly.

"How is David?" I ask to change the subject.

"Bald. But I still love him. You're lucky to have Mark."

"I know."

"Jody," she says, "about the baby—is it all right?"

"Yes. You said I ought to get rid of it."

"Did I? I really don't know what you ought to do, or what I said about the baby." She pours herself another drink. "It's too late now, anyway."

129

We talk a little of death and dying, and Jenny's new-found enthusiasm for reincarnation.

"Two weeks ago I was content, or reasonably so, with the idea that I would *never* know. Now I finally think I understand. And *without* that bolt of lightning I was always crying for." She finishes her drink. "Have your baby and live long and prosper. Happy landings."

"Happy landings." I stand up and kiss her on the cheek. "I'm so glad you came. Are you glad?"

"Absolutely." She puts her arm around me, opens the door for me, and we walk out to the street. "Wake me at seven," she says.

"You still open doors for me."

She smiles. "I always did, didn't I? Why the hell did I always do that? You were such a baby."

I nod. "An incompetent."

"Not a *total* incompetent. What I think is—ready for this one? You had such a non-aggressive nature it was easier for you to drift along letting other people yak and do. Not that you wouldn't, or couldn't take care of yourself. It was just easier. . . . I only charge $25 an hour for this. Oh, look at *me*, Jo. I don't believe I've ever criticized you before. Do you suppose that is significant?"

"Jennifer." I think I might cry. "Why didn't you write when I told you about the melanoma? Or call?"

The dimples vanish. "Oh, Jo," she says at last. "I didn't mean to let you down. You'll never know what your letter did to me. I thought for sure you were going to die, and I knew if you died, I'd never get over it. It was self-preservation."

"Then how did you finally do it? Why *did* you come?"

"Does it matter?"

"To me, yes!"

"Because I love you. I really do. I'm sorry." She starts to cry.

"No, I am sorry. I love you, too." When I tell her I am sorry she looks at me in astonishment. I realize now that Jenny still thinks I am going to die. And she has come here to say . . . what she has just said: Happy landings. *She really thinks I am dying.* I am touched. But what impresses me most is that she came because of it—or perhaps, in spite of it—by way of a farewell. And it is harder for her than for me. Damn. Damn. Damn! I resent it. I am pleased. I am depressed. I am elated. (Ambivalent? Me?) So what do I say now? Denial? Acknowledgement? Reassurance? I haven't the slightest idea. Anyway, I think everything has been said.

"Oh, Jody," Jenny says quietly. Her voice cracks. "You sure scared the hell out of me."

"I scared the hell out of me, too." Indeed.

End of episode.

twenty

THERE ARE, OF COURSE, two sides to this endless routine of hospital tests—one is that I can never get used to these needles sticking into me, the other is that I need the affirmation that everything is still all right.

The lab technician always remains calm and non-commital at this simple mechanical process of drawing blood.

"I need a #18, John," he says to another technician who handles some very large needles.

"I can't find a #18."

"Then give me a #20."

I pray silently that a #20 is not much bigger than a #18.

My Mickey Mouse wristwatch is running again. Reassuring. His orange gloves measure out the minutes and hours. He smiles while the #20 needle descends and punctuates the vein that waits darkly under the pale skin inside my elbow. The blood runs red and frothy into the pyrex tubes.

This vampire is a practically painless sticker. The

vampire (as the lab technicians like to call themselves) releases the tourniquet and marks the spot with a band-aid, and that is that. Until next time.

The mouse smiles. Eleven-thirty. "Hang in there, Mouse," I say out loud.

"Mouse?" says the vampire.

"Have a nice day." I wave and make a graceful exit lest Dracula think I am the kind of lady who talks to her wristwatch.

There is a glorious strong sun. It is nice to be warm. I feel I am something wrapped in a cocoon—it shuts me in; it shuts others out. When will a butterfly emerge from this chrysalis that is me? Vincent Van Gogh wrote to his brother: *"I should like to know what I am the larva of myself."* Me too.

We sit together on the floor—Remy, Chris, Matthew and I, in the "Lotus Posture." Neither I nor Matthew can get our feet "soles up" on our thighs, (Matt's legs are too short and I am too round!) so we sit Indian style. Our goal is "pure consciousness at the highest level of being."

We are somewhat better at controlled breathing, but the boys are a little giddy and spend a lot of time woolgathering. Their deep meditation is flimsy and their intense concentration quite brittle.

"In . . . two . . . three . . . four . . . out . . . two . . . three . . . four . . . hold . . . two . . . three . . . four. . . ."

Mark comes in and sits on the edge of the sofa. He cocks his head and watches us where we sit, and finally says, "What's happening?"

"We're meditating, Daddy," says Remy.

134

"And breathing," adds Chris. "I'm a great big Indian chief. This is my bow and barrow."

"Why?" Mark steps over me on his way to the kitchen.

"Today we breathe," I say. "Tomorrow we chant. And the next day, astral-projection. We're going straight from the eyebrows to the Pleaides. Radhakrishna Radhakrishna Radhakrishna."

"Where? Where are we going, Mama?" Chris jumps up. "Can I come?"

"Straight to the funny farm," says Mark, shaking his head.

"You know," I say as Mark helps me up off the floor, "Jenny was into this stuff a long time ago. Out-of-body experiences and stuff, long before it was popular."

"I'll bet. Jenny always was a little peculiar."

"So are we all. Well, 340 million Hindus do it all the time. Hieronymo's mad againe.—Shantih shantih shantih."

"You don't say." He wanders off into the kitchen. "Where's dinner?"

"I'm replacing my anger, fear, and insecurity with patience, love, and understanding. It's spontaneous mood-making—radiation of Joy. Do you think I'm crazy?"

"I think you've been to the library again." he says. "Next thing you'll be jogging."

No jogging. Lately my idea of strenuous physical fitness stops with sex. My insecurities are coming back. I'm holding on to life as to a shaky *duenna*. Hare Krishna. Hare Rama.

I stand at the window and stare at the half-moon caught in the treetop. I do not doubt the existence of the soul—a non-material body within the material body. Where do these insecurities come from? There is a black hole somewhere in me, swallowing up light. I only worry at night.

135

A siren—an ambulance—shrieks out of the darkness. Then silence. Outside all the houses are dark. Everyone sleeps but me. I hate not being able to sleep, I hate standing here alone in the dark, waiting for morning. I think of Jenny. I see her smile, her delight in life.

I recall a conversation with Beth, my editor and good friend one afternoon. After climbing a flight of stairs to her apartment I discovered her bedridden—I thought she might rather rest, but she asked me in.

"Take me as I am," she said. Half of her bed was littered with manuscripts and books and papers. She was down flat with an attack of thrombo-phlebitis, something she gets regularly since the birth of her daughter in 1946. "I developed a pulmonary embolism," she said. "Very few people recover from a pulmonary embolism. I did. And if I stay down I get over this—at least temporarily, until next time."

She told me of a peculiar experience she had once. "I wasn't really very sick at the time. I had an appendectomy and went into shock—I looked down upon my body, head and all. I had never seen it before except in a mirror, and I felt that I was floating above it somehow. I could see the nurses working, and the doctor running in and working. I couldn't feel a thing, but I saw it all. Then I felt nauseous and everything came back together again. The doctor said, 'She's here, she's come around.' I don't tell this to many people," she said. "The important part is that I experienced a feeling of apartness from my physical self that can only be described as a kind of translation. I felt independent, weightless, unhampered. Yet I was totally objective and knowledgeable. It was not an unpleasant feeling, and although I was not reluctant to return to my body I can well understand why there are those who do not want to return. It was an immortal sensation."

I told Beth, I confided in her, how desperately I love the aches and pleasures of life now that I feel in greatest danger of losing them. I told her how carefully I've NOT been practicing Bach's *Toccata and Fugue*—I think I feel that as long as there are still things unfinished, I will be able to fool death into waiting until I'm ready. 'Sir,' I'll say, (or 'Madame') 'I can't play the middle part yet. The beginning and the end are finished, but I'll need a little more time to practice the middle part.' I know, of course, that the middle is too difficult, and if I had a hundred years to practice I'd never be able to play it. But the absurd Old Man (or Woman) will say, 'All right—another six months. Another year at the most.' *Then.* Only I will carefully continue NOT to practice the middle part.

I told her how I cannot bear to think of killing the mouse that scratches and chews in my bottom cupboard, how I can't bring myself to disturb the round, white sac of eggs a spider has hung in one corner of my ceiling. I can't even swat flies.

"I've been thinking about the book you have in mind," she said. "I'm so glad you're writing again." She took the sample chapter I brought for her. "Push on with it!" And touching my hand, "I look at you and I think, 'Why Jody?' Perhaps because you can take it. I am so proud of you!"

Why Jody? Because. Just because. A hundred 'why's'. A hundred 'becauses.' Why not Jody?

twenty-one

"**M**ARRY ME," I SAID ONCE, in a fever. Never again. Sometimes the effervescence goes flat.

For two weeks Mark has not changed expression—his mouth is cast in an everlasting scowl. "Look," he says tiredly, "I've been working all day and I'm up studying half the night. You sit here all day and play with that damn typewriter and I haven't even got a decent shirt to wear in the morning. I can't wear this. You might as well throw it away." He tosses the shirt into a heap on the floor.

"I'm sorry," I say, wondering who it was put the oil spots on the crummy shirt in the first place. It was not me.

"I like to have clean shirts to wear, that's all I ask."

"I tried to get the spots out. They wouldn't come," I say. "Wear the yellow one instead."

"The yellow one is wrinkled. Don't you even *look* at these before you hang them up?"

139

"I said I was sorry. It looks all right to me."

"Well, it isn't!"

I can feel my backbone stiffening. "I'll do it over."

"Don't bother. I'll wear it wrinkled."

"Damn it!" I say, "I'll do it over!"

He says nothing, then "I'll manage. Why don't you just go pick up the house. It looks like a pig-pen. Can't you manage to have the boys pick up after themselves? I work hard all day. I shouldn't have to come home to *this*." He sighs, runs his fingers along the top of the bookcase and shakes off the dust with his thumb.

It does not matter that I have pulled a mountain of dirty clothes six blocks to the laundromat in a rusty flyer wagon, or that I washed four loads in a machine I had to kick at ten-minute intervals to keep it going. Or that I had to put up with the baby fussing and drooling over a new tooth and Matthew either trying to help or else whining for a soda the whole time. There are toys on the floor, wrinkles in his shirt, and dust on the bookcase.

"The toilet is clogged," he says.

"I know. It has a tennis ball stuck in it."

"A tennis ball? Why don't you watch these kids? That's thirty dollars for a plumber!"

"Maybe you can get it out," I suggest. "I couldn't."

"You'll have to call a plumber first thing in the morning," he says.

"Can you spare all this free advice?" I ask him.

"What do you do all day? Sit around like poor dying Camille and wait for sympathy?" he says.

"I flush tennis balls down the toilet! I stuff socks down the little holes in the washer! I sit on your shirts! What do I do for sympathy?"

"You're missing the point," he says. "I'm only suggesting that you might make better use of your time. Make lists.

140

Budget your time."

"*You* make a list," I say. "*You* call a plumber."

"Is there anything to drink?" he asks.

"There's a couple of cokes in the refrigerator."

"I don't want a coke. What else is there?"

"Milk." I am getting tired of this.

"All right." He pours himself a glass of milk. "This milk is sour," he says, pouring it down the sink. "Why do you continue to shop at that grubby little store when I told you all they sell is old stuff the other stores can't sell. By the way," he says, "I went over your figures in the checkbook today. They're wrong."

"That's possible." My spinal column has fused. Ice creeps up toward my jaw. "I'm no bookkeeper," I say with clenched teeth.

"You're twenty-seven dollars off."

"I'm doing the best I can."

"You've got to take some of the responsibility around here. I can't do everything! Maybe you ought to forget about writing that absurd book and concentrate on money management instead."

"*Money* management? There's none to manage! Maybe if you'd forget about those ridiculous hand-axes and bones and graves, and concentrate on making more money I'd have more practice!"

"All I know is, you're overdrawn, and I don't get paid for another week. I don't know how we'll pay a plumber."

"All right! I did it all on purpose! I messed up the toilet, and I wrinkled your shirt and soured the milk just so I could laugh at you in my sleep, thinking how mad you'd be!" I fling a pencil at him. It grazes his ear and hits the wall behind him. "That's in case you want to add anything else to your damned *list*—mismatched socks or something."

He is surprised. "You could have hurt my eye," he says,

picking up the pencil. He snaps it in two and throws the pieces in the trash.

"You can go to hell," I say. "I resign. I never wanted to be a bookkeeper anyway." I jerk the door open, trembling with rage, and slam it behind me—on the fingers of my left hand. I am too angry to feel any pain, but outside under the street light, I see all the fingers are swollen and bleeding. Damn. Now I've probably managed to break all my stupid fingers besides. It will give him something else to rave about. The rage is worse than the pain, but my fingers will not bend.

How dare he speak to me like that? In three months I may be dead. He'll be sorry when I'm dead. I picture him weeping, unconsoled in guilty remorse, head in his hands, repeating my name and wild with grief. I am glad. He'll wish he'd never—*what's wrong with me?* What am I thinking? I can't believe that just came out of my head. This is absurd.

Why doesn't he cherish me, treasure me, touch me with reverence and awe?

Reverence and awe. Good Lord, who do I think I am, God? Wonderwoman? The Girl of the Golden West? But if he thought I was dying he would be nicer.

He's treating me as if I am a normal, healthy, real person. I ought to be glad. Then why this absurd flood of tears? Because he does not care. He doesn't even care. I'll never come back, ever.

I walk and walk until I am too exhausted to walk any farther. My shoe has come untied and my fingers are too stiff to retie it, so it flaps along, fwap, fwap, fwap, fwap,

fwap on the sidewalk. And finally, there's no place to go anyway, except home.

Reverence and awe. I am apalled. What's happening to me? Do I really sit around like poor dying Camille and wait for sympathy?

Mark is asleep. I look at him for a few minutes, hoping he'll wake up and tell me how glad he is I'm home, how sorry he is, and what a clod he's been. He mumbles something I can't understand. For a minute I think he will wake and say something . . . but he takes a deep breath and sleeps on. He doesn't even know I'm here.

Taking my pillow, I put my hand to the door and close it softly after me. I will sleep on the couch until he apologizes.

I sleep on the couch for four nights, and nothing is said. Then it is over. My fingers aren't broken after all. Nor is my heart. And that is all there is to it. I decide not to be angry. Anger is something I can control.

I take all the anger, all my guilts, my fears, failures, frustrations, mentally wrap them together in a tight bundle and flush them down the john with the tennis ball. It helps. I feel better. I settle, quite comfortably, for accepting myself just as I am, neither God nor Wonderwoman, but a normal, healthy (as far as I know) human being a little lower than an angel.

Whoever said it was going to be roses all the way?

twenty-two

I USED TO WONDER HOW
and why I am ME, myself, and not someone else—and why
not as easily a fish, or a cat, or a tree?

Doctor Lewis Thomas writes in *The Lives of a Cell,*

> Statistically, the probability of any one of us being here
> is so small that you'd think the mere fact of existing would
> keep us all in a contented dazzlement of surprise. We are
> alive against the stupendous odds of genetics, infinitely
> out-numbered by all the alternates who might, except for
> luck, be in our places. . . .
>
> Everyone is one in three billion at the moment, which
> describes the odds. Each of us is a self-contained, free-
> standing individual, labeled by specific protein configura-
> tions at the surface of cells, identifiable by whorls of
> fingertip skin, maybe even by special medleys of fragrance.
> You'd think we'd never stop dancing.

All in all, I think simply being alive is a miraculous achievement. When I woke this morning, I thought of the tremendous change in my life once the powerful catalytic agent CANCER was introduced. I've come to feel a certain indifference to the few dark horrors that my mind occasionally offers up. Things go on. No one on earth can give me a signed and notarized certificate saying I haven't still got this damned disease. But I can adapt. Every change requires some re-ordering to accommodate it. And I find a certain tenacious peace-of-mind in prayer—not as a greedy child whining to an indulgent parent, nor as a beggar, but as a sort of opening up of cosmic pathways into my mind.

A note I discover among some old papers: Adversity helps men to rise above themselves.

Is that true? *I think so.*

•　　•　　•　　•

A comet that has traveled eons around uncounted suns has met its end here. Tonight there is supposed to be a 'spectacular' meteor shower, the result of the comet's dramatic demise.

We pop corn and spread our blankets across the front yard grass at midnight and lie flat out with the earth spinning under us and the stars spinning above. Where is everybody? Tucked away in their beds, no doubt. We ought to run through the streets, banging on the doors, crying at the locks, "You're missing the show!"

There is no moon. I am reminded of scorching summer

nights at the beach where Mark and I walked hand in hand, trying not to scare the sandpipers in their dark search for sandcrabs, and stepping carefully around the dozens of silent bodies entwined on blankets, making love, as unaware of us as if we were invisible.

There is the Big Dipper. Gemini and Antila on the horizon. Mark explains to the boys how they might find Polaris in the northern sky if they are ever lost at sea, or alone in the woods. "Polaris is the brightest yellow star at the end of the handle of the Little Dipper. First find the two pointer stars in the Big Dipper," he says. "Can you find them?"

"There they are!" says Chris, looking in another direction.

"Polaris is right at the North Celestial Pole, so it is the most important navigational star."

"That's where Santa Claus lives with all God's angels," Chris tells Matthew.

"I wish I had a book on stars," Remy says.

Cosmic immensities perplex me. I grope to define undefinables, to participate in the insistent solidity of rocks, in the unfamiliar air and inviolable patterns of cells and fossils, in the enormous silences of stars. I hear "it" as a deaf person "hears" music by touching a radio and feeling the vibrations.

We share the popcorn and the binoculars. The show *is* spectacular. A skyful of blazing trails, tailed lights and erratic clusters of ice and dust.

Finally the boys sleep, salt and popcorn crumbs on their lips, perhaps dreaming of comets and polestars. I hope so. Mark and I lie together in full possession of the grandeur and solitude.

"When you think of the vastness and enormity of the universe, and of the billions and billions of planets and stars, doesn't it make you feel small and insignificant?" he says.

Then he adds, "Me neither!"

. . . .

The Fourth of July, a day of purest sizzling gold, of hot dogs and cold watermelon in the grass, lemonades and Eskimo pies, wax mustaches and cannon blasts; wading in the creek in water so clear and cold it makes your teeth ache; an evening of fireworks. Enchanted children, barefoot and sunburnt, write their names with sparklers in the summer dark. Fire-flowers bloom in the night driveways, bottle-rockets whistle up the sky and fade. Fountains of fire fly up and breaking, drip showers of red, white, and blue.

I thought that nothing would ever be the same again, and it's true. I indulge in the exaltation of being ALIVE. I know my life has value—to me, to others. I am loved by the people I love. I feel pure elation at the changing seasons. What a marvel is this world we live in! What a marvel is this whirling, clockwork universe! That we are, in fact, spinning like a Fourth-of-July pinwheel at incredible veloc- ities. We live in the neighborhood of Perseus, and Auriga, and Orion, and toward the center of our galaxy lies the great starcloud of Sagittarius. I want to shout to the people picnicing on the grass, "Open your eyes! This is our *home*! Cry out with joy at quiet seeds that bloom into radishes and roses and any of a thousand other species of fruit or flower. Wonder at protozoan life swarming out of summer ponds.

Stand amazed at the formless shifting of sea and sand, at the exquisitely patterned rhythms that regulate the heartbeat and the genes. Admire the powers of the minds, that times and places and people long past move *now* along the thin and curious threads of the brain, a myriad of cherished memories. Delight in the sunlight, in the cricket's piping, in the sparrow's madrigals. There is no time for bitterness, no time to be bored!"

•   •   •   •

A fierce wind comes up in the night with a roar that rattles the windows and doors. I can't sleep. I am too tense. I turn on the TV to the late show, which is *The Caine Mutiny*, with Humphrey Bogart and Van Johnson, but I can't concentrate on the story for the wind. I have seen the movie anyway. I curl up in the chair and listen while the wind blows waves of anxiety over me. When I was a child, I would curl up in bed under three blankets, covering my ears against the howling wind outside. We could tell, by wind-clouds piling up along the tops of the Sierra-Nevadas, when there would be a big blow. The wind always came from the west, blowing sand into waves of dunes in the front yard, settling a fine, thick slit on the window sills and in the corners. Sand blasted the paint off cars and pitted windows and blotted out the sun. It stung our eyes and textured our dinner and turned tumbleweeds into flying missiles.

Once, the circus came to town in the middle of a terrific windstorm. Their Big Top swayed and groaned, the ropes and posts and canvases snapped like ships in the blowing sand. The daring young men on the flying trapeze may have been daring, but they were not fools, so they stayed safely on the ground while their swings billowed and lifted without them. Still, we saw monkeys and elephonts, lion-tamers and clowns. We saw Bambi-the-Snake-Woman, and Bobo-the-Dog-Faced-Boy. The Man-Turned-To-Stone invited our hands to feel the vibrations on his leg while he spoke. A nine-foot giant mummy, leathery and brown, reclined in a wood-and-glass case. Beside him in a smaller case there was another mummy of an ancient infant that looked like a little shriveled, brown monkey.

And I remember once, Gypsies camped their tents and wagons at the far end of our lot. Someone said Gypsies stole children, dyed their skins brown with the juice of berries and walnuts, and they had to be Gypsies for the rest of their lives. I lived in horror they might kidnap me, yet I secretly hoped they would, so that I could live a life traveling in tents, wearing gold earrings and bracelets up to my elbows, and dancing to the music of accordians and tambourines. However, I took the long, round-about way to school for as long as they camped there. I never heard one tambourine.

In school every morning, they gave us mimeographed pictures to color of Farmer Brown, Farmer Brown's Wife, and Farmer Brown's Boy Bill. (Never once Gypsies!)

I remember the hills and gullies full of sage and creosote and cactus, coyotes and rattlesnakes and lizards. My brother used to catch horned-toads and put them in popsicle-stick corrals and pretend they were his "horses." When more and more people began to move in, they all vanished. The shrill night howling of coyotes used to send shivers up and down my back. Now most of the remaining coyotes are pacing in zoos, although the sheepmen say some still attack and kill their sheep. I suffer with the sheep, but my heart is with the coyotes. I think the whole history of creation is in those sheep and the coyotes.

The wind continues to howl like a pack of coyotes at the windows. When I wake at dawn, the TV is still on, though it's dumb and blind.

twenty-three

I GATHER UP THE LAST of the folded laundry—mostly diapers, and stack it in the wagon. Since the car was repossessed we travel by horse and cart, minus the horse, of course. I drag the wagon up the hill toward home, thinking it must be a hundred degrees in the shade. I catch a glimpse of myself reflected in the glass of a store window as I pass. My hair is wet with sweat and it flies wildly around my head like electric wires. My cheeks are flushed. Somewhere in this grotesque body, like the baby I carry, there is a small, delicate, beautiful person that is also me, trapped, imprisoned in flesh and sweat and maternity smocks.

"I think I can, I think I can," I chant aloud, remembering the Little Engine That Could. The throbbing twinge in my back has gotten steadily worse. A sharp pain circles my body like a vise. I pull the wagon into the shade and flop down on the diapers to wait for it to let go. It passes. I think I can, I think I can.

"Jody? Where've you been?" Mark comes down the stairs and bends to help me unload the wagon. He bounds back up the stairs.

"To London," I say, "to visit the Queen. Obviously."

"Jennifer is here," he yells down to me.

"I think I can." The stairs are Everest. "I think I can," I chant, not hearing what he says. He holds the door for me.

"Hi ya!" Jenny hugs me hello. "Damn it, Jo, what have you been doing?"

"Climbing mountains," I say, kissing her cheek. She smells of perfume. Her hair has just been done. Her nails are perfect and polished. I am delighted. "What are you doing here?"

"I just dropped by to see if everything's all right."

"Everything's all right," Mark says, filling three glasses with ice and pouring water in them.

"Why aren't you in New York? I thought you were doing Albee off-Broadway."

"Oh, yes." She drops onto the sofa beside me. Would you believe I quit another show?"

"You quit! Why?"

"I was tired of it all. I couldn't stand the adolescent director—he was young enough for pimples! He had us holding hands, walking around in the dark, jumping off tables into each other's arms. 'Learn to trust each other,' he said. 'Be a team!' 'I trust you,' I said, 'I'll be glad to be in your play, but I'll be damned if I'll play these ridiculous games! What does all this have to do with Albee?'"

"So you quit."

"I quit. What really gets me," Jenny says, "is that they didn't even beg me to stay."

The pain is worse. It etches itself in concentric circles from the small of my back outward. I drop my glass.

154

"Hey, are you okay?" Jenny says, scooping ice off the carpet.

"I'm sorry. I'm tired," I say. "I think I need a little nap."

"Go ahead," she says, fluffing a pillow and tucking it under my head. "We'll take care of the kids, and dinner."

"I'll just rest a minute—" I lie quietly on my back and close my eyes.

I must be dreaming. It is ten years ago. Mark revs up his motorcycle. It sputters and roars, and a strong salt wind whips my hair far out behind. I clutch Mark's middle with my knees and wrap my arms tight around him. Together we ride, flying, flying. The summer sky is a soft gentian blue.

A second motorcycle swerves past us. The long-haired boy riding it shouts something to us, but it is lost in the wind, leaving only an echo. He rounds a corner, and a bus he had not counted on screeches to a halt, too late. The boy lies in the street, convulsing in the middle of his broken bike. Blood runs out of his mouth and nose, pouring into the street in crooked, lengthening rivers. I am sick. Great waves of panic leave me shivering all over, banging my teeth together. I double over and vomit all over my shoes. The pavement wavers, rises up and hits my nose.

I breathe deeply. My back is cramped, and I feel nauseous. I've been time-traveling again. My panic disappears. I'll go back now, and sleep a little longer. I travel farther.

It must be getting very late. The western sky is reddening the clouds of white dust the sheep have raised. My cousin

155

Ginger and I have picked armfuls of buttercups and yellow asters, and we can't hold any more. Ginger is eight, dark and brown. I am four, pale and blonde. We never see the sheepherder we follow, but his little dog runs ahead of us barking at the sheep. We walk slowly, following behind and picking wildflowers. We cross the railroad tracks. We swing on a long wooden gate that creaks and bends when we climb on it. It hangs loose on the high posts of the empty sheep corral. We walk slowly along beside the train tracks. I am forbidden to play here.

The wind blows. I can smell the flowers, I can feel the heat as the sun curls down.

"This way," Ginger calls.

But every way looks the same to me. It is all dust and brush and sky, and one way is like another. I run, and all the flowers I picked scatter around my feet.

"Wait! This way!" Ginger calls.

But I can't hold myself here. I can't stop running. Lizards run out of the bushes and their tails leave little winding trails in the sand. Ginger tries to pick up the flowers I dropped, but there are too many of them.

The red sunset is accompanied by bats from the foothills. They whirl and dive in quiet circles over my head. *Bats get in your hair!* I cry out in fright, and warm water swirls out and runs down my legs. I dance around, running and turning. The fluid is under enormous pressure and will not stop. It flows.

I wake abruptly, and notice I lie in a puddle of water. Where has everybody gone? "Mark?" I shout.

The membranes have ruptured. I reach for the telephone to dial Annelise's number. Before it rings, I hang up and call Doctor Sontag instead.

156

"Doctor's out to lunch," says the voice at the answering service. "He'll be in at two o'clock."

I leave my name and number and check the clock. One twenty. Another pain rips through me.

"Mark!" I can envision Mark pulling me ten blocks to the hospital in the old flyer wagon.

Jennifer bursts into the apartment, carrying a large red-and-white paper bag of fried chicken. Mark follows, carrying another bag. He turns pale. "What is it?"

"I've already called the doctor." I say. "He's out to lunch. I'll be all right." As I say this, the pain explodes again.

"She should be in the hospital," Jenny says, watching me ease myself off the sofa.

"Shall we go by wagon," I say, half-joking, "or would you prefer to take turns carrying me pig-a-back?"

"This is ridiculous," Jenny sputters.

"We'll borrow Annelise's car," Mark says coolly. "I've already talked to her about it. It's fine."

"Where are the boys?" I try to keep calm.

"Annelise has them."

"Annelise?" I am horribly aware of a jealous gnawing inside me. It wraps itself around me and squeezes, a python out of a basket. My eyes fill with tears. So long, gang. Ciao. Lonely, fluttering, shrill Annelise. Oh God, I pray, if I die let it not be Annelise, with her padded bosom and painted smile.

"Have you a bag packed to take to the hospital?" Jenny says gaily. "Why don't I pack a few things for you. A toothbrush, a comb—"

"That would be fine," I say. I hate hospitals.

It is no distance at all. I could have walked it easily had I not been so out of control of my body. But I realize that I am glad for the ride, even in Annie's car. Reconciled, I think of Annie spreading peanut butter on bread for the next fifteen years. Why not? With a little time and practice she'll be a wonderful mother. I can almost laugh. Almost. As long as I can keep a sense of humor everything will be fine.

The doctor inserts a gloved hand from my gizzle to my sash. "She's dilated to five. I'll be downstairs if you need me," he says with a snap of the rubber glove as he removes it.

"Please don't go," I say after the pain passes. "It's happening too fast. I can't stop it." I am shaking.

"It will be a while yet," the nurse announces indulgently, patting my hand. Damn her.

The door slides shut behind them. I lie very rigid, filled with incomprehensible pain. Relax, I think. Relax. I pulse with the steady bump-bump, bump-bump of the fetal heartbeat coming from the monitoring machine. The sound becomes a part of me, a sort of chant, a song—bump-bump, bump-bump, bump-bump, one rhythm, rising or falling in pitch, but constant. Damn them all. So, it is you and me, babe. Here we are, alone together. Full speed ahead.

It's my duty to tell you. They say you may be *impaired*. Impaired, with strange eyes and a strange smile. The pain is real. This is earth. I don't pretend to understand it all, I tell him, but earth is a place of mistakes. If you are less than perfect, I'm sorry. Know that I very much wanted you to be perfect and beautiful. I love you anyway.

I'm listening, hums the heartbeat from the monitor.

I love you—eyes, hands, whorl of hair at the crowning, wrinkles at the ankles and elbows, big toes, little toes, I love you. I'm sorry if I have to die. I'm sorry if I have let you down.

I am listening, he says.

158

I must mention the screams. I had decided to be very quiet and dignified this one last time, to savor the experience, to pay attention, but I realize with detachment that the screams I hear are mine. Oh well.

Where is the doctor, with his shining tools and his sterile green gown? Where are the nurses with their needles and analgesics and anesthetics? Where is Mark? I might as well be squatting in a tent in the middle of the Gobi desert. Something is wrong. I ring for the nurse. I never expected this much pain. This primitive, pushing body is mine. This whole primitive process is splitting me in two, I am tearing from the inside out—

—the baby emerges at once, wet and white and crying spontaneously, covered with long streaks of blood. The afterbirth is dumped unceremoniously beside him. I am bleeding all over the sheets. I sit up and take the baby in my arms. The umbilical cord pulsates less and less and finally quits. I check out his fingers and toes, genitals and ears and all. He seems perfect. What a miracle! We rock and I whisper to him hoarsely, "Little lamb, who made thee?"

The nurse arrives, takes one startled look at us, and gasps. A second nurse arrives, followed by Doctor Sontag, who is followed by Mark. We need only a drummer, a couple of trumpets and a baton twirler for fanfare.

"Well, aren't you the sneaky one," the doctor says cleverly.

The nurse would take the baby from me, but I hold onto him and we continue to rock and sing. I am furious that no one was here with me. But I have found a strength that surprises me. I did it all by myself. I can do anything. Like

159

Jonah, I have been swallowed by Leviathan, and came out alive after all. I can do *anything*!

Mark's arms are suddenly around me and I press my face into his shoulder. "It's another boy," I whisper.

"Yes. Shall I call your folks and tell them?" he says.

"I'll do it."

"A boy," says Doctor Sontag. "So, You're still the Queen Bee!"

August eighth. Today we have another son. Seven pounds of pink flesh, a special kind of softness. Five little boys! He looks just like his brothers, but he is a totally new person, absolutely unique. In all the whole history of the world there has never been another like him. He is perfect and healthy. He nurses vigorously. We've named him Marc Ariel.

Today I am like an apple—deep inside me, like a star of five dark seeds, there is a cool, sweet peace.

. . . .

Jennifer's suitcase is packed, her hair is done, her plane ticket to California is bought. All that remains is for her to go out the front door and down the stairs. All night we have talked about old things and new things in drowsy voices, until dawn. We smiled so much.

The baby cries. Jenny picks him up gingerly and holds him against her. He cries again, hunting for a breast that will satisfy his hunger. She kisses his forehead, his waving fists, his feet. Her lips rest for a moment on his cheek. She looks as if she might cry as she brings him to me. I slip down one side of my blouse, giving him my breast. He quiets, roots around for a moment, and sucks contentedly.

"Well. If I don't move my ass I'll miss my flight." Jenny lifts her suitcase.

"Jenny, we'll miss you."

Now she does cry. "I'll write every Christmas, and call if I'm drunk. Or pregnant. I really want another baby. I've missed out on so much."

"I've loved having you here."

She sits down beside me on the sofa, looking at the baby as if she wants to hold him again, her hands empty. "It's not easy to go."

"It never is," I tell her.

We sit, reluctant to say the last words. "Well. Wish me luck!" Jenny kisses me quickly, and then all the children. She hugs Mark, takes her suitcase, and is gone. The door closes with a soft thud.

•　　•　　•　　•

Two A.M. I wake out of a deep, drenched sleep. The telephone keeps ringing and ringing.

"Jody!" Jenny's voice, ebullient. It has been three months since she left and I have not heard from her. "Wonderful news!"

"Jenny," I say. "What is it?" A slat of moonlight falls through a crack in the curtain onto the phone.

"I auditioned for a CBS affiliate for weather girl and newscaster—the man said newscasting is where it's really going to be at for women. I sent them tapes of some of my old commercials, and he called me back! They loved me!"

"That's wonderful," I tell her. "That's really wonderful!"

161

Except—I'm, pregnant!" She cries into the telephone. "I'll be FAT!"

"Are you glad? Or—what?"

"David is ecstatic. I only wonder, why *now*? They won't want me fat. Oh Jody, why can't I have it *all*? I'll never have this chance again. And I want it all. What am I going to do!"

I really don't know. Nothing is perfect.

twenty-four

THANKSGIVING MORNING comes with a smell of bacon frying in the skillet, and cinnamon and hot chocolate, and a crunch of walnuts for the dressing. The turkey is stuffed and roasting in the oven by nine.

Remy has found a half-frozen katy-did to add to his "zoo," a fruit-jar collection of the last of autumn's grasshoppers and crickets.

"Put the katy-did away and run and wash. Grandma and Grandpa will be here any time now."

"They already are!" he yells.

We run out to meet them, putting our arms about their necks and kissing them.

"Wow! Let me look at you!"

"I'm glad you finally made it."

"Did you think we wouldn't?"

"Where'd all those white hairs come from, Susie?" Papa has called me "Susie" for as long as I can remember.

"It's heredity, Papa!" I say.

Mama is very small and slender—almost girlish. Her hair is tied back in a chignon. She holds my hand tightly. Mama is stronger than we imagined. I think we are stronger than we imagine.

I have been close to my mother, but we never talked much about things intimate or personal. I carry her inborn reserve. The minor problems of adolescence, boys, pimples, the first menstruation, the first brassiere—all great embarrassments to me—were taken care of quickly and with a minimum of fuss, and I kept my feelings to myself. She has always been there if I needed her. She never understood my revulsion at the dresses and pretty clothes she wanted me to wear when I wore faded blue jeans and too-large T-shirts, or why I let my hair go long and wild and stayed by myself, obstinate and sullen and full of unshared fantasies. I never meant to be rude or rebellious, but I was. I never felt unloved.

We know each other better now than we ever have before because we are no longer afraid to share.

And dear, dear Papa, living on one side of Mama and I on the other. We have never really connected—not yet. But I know he loves me, and oh, how I love him.

Thanksgiving isn't the way it used to be when Ginger and I hid behind the steaming stove and stole celery sticks with cheese, and apples, and fingers of whipped cream off the pies. There is no great explosion of uncles and aunts and cousins by the dozens. I have not seen Ginger since Grandma's funeral ten years ago, and we have not all been together for Thanksgiving for many a year longer. Sometimes when it's hot and still, I listen for sounds that will take me back home. We have come so far into the years that the memory almost gives up trying.

We exchange hugs and kisses. Such excitement. Everyone is cheerful. The boys clap their hands and stand on tip-toe and catapult like rabbits, never staying in one place longer than a few seconds.

The day is what we make it, full of bright inner still-lifes and remembrances. Matthew sits on Papa's lap, wearing Papa's eyeglasses far down on his nose, while Papa magically produces a handful of special rocks he has brought for this occasion.

"This is quartz, limestone, mica, and iron pyrite," he says to the boys. "Fool's Gold. This is fossil wood, and fossil bone." He chips away at one of the rocks and cracks it open. "Tourmaline crystals!"

"I have an Indian arrowhead," Remy produces a box of his treasures, "and a katy-did."

"Do you have any gold, Grandpa?" asks Chris.

"Gold isn't easy to find, even for an old rock-hound like me," says Papa.

"Tell us about the Tommyknockers, Grandpa."

They are lost in a world of crystal and agate, gloryholes in the ground, mines and the Tommyknockers who haunt them.

Mama peels the potatoes and spices the pumpkin pies with nutmeg and cloves. I feel a surge of joy, a homecoming. "I remember the Thanksgiving you forgot to put the pumpkin in the pumpkin pies!"

"And the time I put the pudding in the cupboard instead of the oven!"

"I can tell my keen mind is also inherited!"

My brother Gary comes with his wife and their children, bringing a shock of cold air through the front door, flinging coats and scarves and caps on beds and chairs. The children squeal prisms of laughter, and puffing out their cheeks, they crunch peanuts and drop shells and chase one another in and out of the forest of adult legs. They dance around the kitchen full of steam and roast turkey and cranberries and brown gravy, candied yams with marshmallows and pumpkin pies.

"What are we thankful for?" Papa says.

Everybody has something to offer. "For turkeys and pie!"

"I'm thankful for ME!"

"That I can come on earth and be in a family."

"For Heavenly Father and Jesus."

"For cinnamon toast and hot chocolate."

"P.U. I hate chocolate." Chris holds his nose and pokes out his tongue.

"Since when?"

"Since now. My stomach aches."

"I'm grateful for my family, the Church, and then for my job."

"I'm grateful for the delight I've had in my children and my grandchildren."

"I'm grateful that the family circle remains unbroken, that we're here together."

"For time," I add. "For the realities of life. For joy."

By mid-afternoon the valley whitens under a dusting of the first snowfall of the season. The troops eat, and stuffed to the ears, they march from the table. Papa winds his watch and lets the little children hear it tick. Mark switches off the lights. Dusk comes early now. We sit together, haloed with visions and glowing fragments of a day almost lost to comprehension, deep inhalations and drowsy eyelids. The baby wakens, nurses, and sleeps again in my arms.

Outside the storm continues. Inside all the light is soft and flickering. Mark says, "All I need now is a little egg nog, a little music, and a lot of lovin'." He smiles a delighted smile, picks up his guitar and plays, singing:

The Owl and the Pussycat went to sea
In a beautiful pea-green boat:
They took some honey and plenty of money
Wrapped up in a five-pound note.

The Owl looked up to the stars above,
And sang to a small guitar,
'Oh, lovely Pussy, Oh Pussy my love,
What a beautiful Pussy you are!

From the darkening window I see sunflowers along the roads and in the empty lots. They have broken and dried and blown away in a cyclone of seeds. The explosion of cold strips the leaves from the trees and flings them into the sky like yellow birds. Autumn has come and gone. The snow piles up in the yard and nests in the trees. Everything is cut of ice and cold. Snow grows out of the avalanched leaves and dry grass and dead flowers, white upon white upon white.

A sparrow flies past the window, small, greedy, and cold. Is he looking in? They are used to my throwing out ends of bread and birdseed—and today I have neglected them. The flock spins off into the wind.

This is an anniversary for me, a sort of birthday. It has been a year.

What a new person I have become. I still read the obituaries first—old habits are hard to break. Sometimes the old dragons still roam. I haven't forgotten the anguish of the event that prompted this growth, nor the long midnight hours of heartache. I think of it every day. But I no longer brood over it. Except for the interminable check-ups every third month, and the x-rays and blood tests, I have eclipsed that event which brought me here. I am alive.

This has been a time of homecoming. If I'd had a choice, I would have chosen not to host this hidden battle. I am a cowardly soldier, shy and unwarlike. But I know now that there is wisdom in tears. Pain does come from darkness, and it *is* pain. Sometimes it is also wisdom.

Today I watched as Christopher learned to tie his shoes —the frustration and anger, the tears, the knots—and the ultimate satisfaction with the perfect bows at his feet. I would not have tied them for him and spoiled his triumph by protecting him from the tears for anything in the world.

Whatever happens next year, or in the year after that, or if I should die tomorrow, I know that my success is not measured by the number of my years on this small planet. Jesus died at thirty-three. So did Alexander the Great. Shelley was barely thirty, Lord Byron was thirty-six and Dylan Thomas was thirty-nine. Here someone will surely say, "But George Bernard Shaw was ninety-four!" *So it goes.*

I respect each hour. I have learned not to waste my time in futile lethargy. It's a good world and a good life. We are Voyagers and Explorers. All our lives are a journey homeward. Our passage is lighted with the dust of comets and nebulae and pulsing stars. Symphonies of milkweed burst around us. Crickets fiddle ancient runes under the stones at our feet. Somewhere in this mystery of motion and sound lie the answers to the enigmas of breath, of plasma and electron, cell and gene. And I wonder, at what point do the things of earth become things of the spirit? I have just begun.

So, this is a portrait of a birth. The butterfly is finally emerging. The book is finished, and I am painfully anxious that it be good. I stayed up until two or three in the morning for weeks trying to finish the final draft. Now I need to move on to something else. Maybe I'll just think in iambic pentameter for awhile. Maybe I'll write another book, a children's book this time.

I am full. Let me stay like this forever, lullabyed by family, by friends, by an unrolling of irrevocable love and intoxicant life. I hold it as carefully as mortal fingers will allow. *Thanks.*

Everything is as it should be, and nothing will change, not ever, I tell myself. Encircled by sleepy children, Mark sings:

> And hand in hand on the edge of the sand
> They danced by the light of the moon, the moon,
> They danced by the light of the moon.

But knowing how things do change, if it should turn out otherwise—well. In the words of a 16th century poet: "Upon my buried body, lie lightly gentle earth."

Peace. OM.